"Tyrone? This is Elaine."

Ten in the morning and he had been awakened by the phone.

"I want to give you something. Remember the card you took from your mother's purse? I still have it. I didn't put it back. I thought you might want it."

Her tone was wistful, wheedling, the whine of the loser, but it was like music in his ears. He swung his feet to the floor and sat on the edge of the bed. He wanted to do this right. He wanted to leave Fox River clean, with no one able to figure out where he had gone. Then he had it. Of course. Elaine could take her last ride in the St. Hilary's minibus.

"...a competent addition to the Father Dowling series."

—Publishers Weekly

"...it's always fun to be with Father Dowling and his busybody housekeeper, Marie Murkin."

—Chicago Sun-Times

Other Father Dowling titles available from Worldwide Mystery by

RALPH McINERNY

JUDAS PRIEST
FOUR ON THE FLOOR
ABRACADAVER

RALPH McINERNY

DESERT SINNER

TORONTO • NEW YORK • LONDON
AMSTERDAM • PARIS • SYDNEY • HAMBURG
STOCKHOLM • ATHENS • TOKYO • MILAN
MADRID • WARSAW • BUDAPEST • AUCKLAND

For Bruce and Laila Fingerhut

DESERT SINNER

A Worldwide Mystery/December 1994

First published by St. Martin's Press, Incorporated.

ISBN 0-373-26158-6

Printed in U.S.A.

"Golden lads and girls all must,
As chimney-sweepers, come to dust."
—Shakespeare, *Cymbeline*

ONE

ELAINE WAITED for what seemed five minutes, then took the stairs. It was five flights down to street level, but she didn't mind—it was better than waiting. Wide, granite, noisy under her heels, the stairs wound down around two elevators that all too visibly and with gravity-defying slowness ascended and descended. The cars were wrought-iron cages which Elaine rode daily without qualm, but seen now from these stairs—great looping cables hanging beneath, a single steel braid stretching tautly into darkness, the greased vertical runners—they seemed as dangerous as a roller coaster. One car passed her going down, of course; she would have bet on that. But moments later she reached the great lobby beneath the rotunda, its floor a checkerboard of dark and white marble. Elaine moved across it at an angle, as if she were on her way to crown a king.

She pushed through the revolving doors into an April noonday with the sun standing high in a pale blue cloudless sky. A breeze carried the scent of spring and youth and fresh beginnings. In any other season Fox River's beauty was largely in the eye of the beholder, but today the city seemed objectively lovely. Her hand rose in a protective salute as she pretended to look toward the park. But then in peripheral vision she saw him. He came to the bottom of the flight of granite steps and looked up at her.

Click. In the microsecond that their eyes met, she took her first snapshot. How many rolls of mental film would she take before her lunch hour was over and she went back to her job in the courthouse? With him she acted like a teenager. A woman thirty-two years old, and don't you forget it, not knowing whether it was better being with him or recalling it afterward, letting the pictures develop behind her closed eyes. Why did she think of them as stills rather than as moving pictures? Maybe because moving pictures had sound and they didn't do much talking, she and Gordon.

He came toward her up the courthouse steps but the noontime crowd was going down and he had to get out of the way, out of sight. She moved to the side to grasp the railing and then he came into view again. Click, to preserve his worried expression, and then, click, to get the look of relief. His hand reached for hers and pressed it before they turned and walked hand in hand at high noon up the street to lunch.

"The Great Wall?"

She turned to smile her assent.

Their favorite place. Eat Chinese. Stamp out rodents. His joke, only he didn't mean it.

"I think I was born on the wrong continent, Elaine. I love rice."

Fried rice. Shrimp fried rice. Always the same. Plus an egg roll. And lots of hot tea. The Great Wall was always crowded at noon, and noisy, which would have been a nuisance if they had talked much, but just being together seemed enough for him too. It didn't seem odd at all to just sit across from him and stare. His slight smile never went away, making a slight dimple in his right cheek. It was impossible not to compare him with poor Walter Nickles, about whom she shuddered to think she had been becoming fatalistic, not quite formulating the thought that he was all she could really expect if she were to find a husband at all. That was more or less the unspoken bargain she'd been making with herself. There wasn't anything wrong with Walter. There were many things right about him. Elaine had even made lists, which she then scrutinized with a cold eye, not wanting to attribute any trait to Walter that he did not truly possess. So severe was her appraisal that justice dictated adding to rather than subtracting from the list. There was no doubt about it. Walter was in so many ways a good man.

She liked him. She admired him. It was easy to imagine fates worse than life with Walter. But there was no magic there, no spark, no leap of the heart that would have made such calculating activities as list-making unnecessary. Elaine scarcely knew what it was that was lacking in Walter. Whatever it was, she had not found it with any other man either. Only while reading or watching a movie did she experience it vicariously and become for a moment the actress, the character, who was drawn to her man as to a magnet. Without that mindless magic, marriage would be an embarrassment. To think of herself in bed with Walter, and of course that is where married couples ended up, was either comic or humiliating. She would be terribly self-conscious but not, she guessed, half as awkward as Walter. It would be like undressing for the doctor.

Now, unexpectedly and without warning, Gordon Jenkins had come and Elaine knew what had been missing from her life. She made no lists of Gordon's traits. Her attraction to him was what a woman's attraction to a man should be, a matter of feeling and emotion, of being swept along rather than doing anything. How silly it would be to wonder what making love with Gordon would be like. As well wonder where a storm came from or what unstoppable force now turned the world green and sent sap pushing through root and branch to bud and leaf. A woman's love for a man was equally a force of nature. Elaine felt borne along on a tumultuous current. And she loved it. She loved Gordon.

She had been squeezing the red paper napkin but now her fingers stole toward his. He turned his hand over and their palms met and Elaine felt such a roaring in her ears she thought she might faint. I am thirty-two years old, she reminded herself, trying to be stern, but her age seemed hilariously funny, just irrelevant with Gordon's fingers entwined with hers.

Only in Trollope could so innocent a gesture as holding hands seem so impossibly erotic. She might have been surrendering herself to him there among the sounds of tableware, the voices of strangers, the scents of tea and rice. They went hand in hand back to the courthouse steps where she shook her head when he offered to go up with her. She leaned toward him and he received her kiss with open eyes. She turned and clattered up the stairs as if she had announced her engagement to the whole of Fox River.

CAPTAIN KEEGAN wasn't back from lunch yet. More likely than not he was at the St. Hilary rectory with Father Dowling. She had been surprised to find a professional policeman so devout, though she suspected he went to the noon mass as often as he did in the hope of being asked to stay for lunch at the rectory. Father Dowling and Captain Keegan went way back, that was his explanation. Elaine had tried to strike up a conversation about the two old friends with Marie Murkin, the parish housekeeper, but the older woman turned frosty as if she were bound by the seal of the confessional, for heaven's sake. Now Elaine was less surprised. She did not care to tell anyone about Gordon either—not Walter, of course, but not anyone else either. She would be as shocked as Marie Murkin if the housekeeper asked her about Gordon.

At her computer, she called up the report she was working on. Her task was to turn into civil prose Captain Keegan's angrily dictated response to Chief

Robertson. What would people think if they knew of all the bickering and disagreement in the Fox River police department. Walter hadn't been at all interested. Their conversations, if you could call them that, centered on his own work as a salesman. When he first told her he was in sales, Elaine had just stared, trying to imagine Walter persuading anyone to buy anything.

"Telesales," he added, as if expecting her reaction. "I work entirely by phone."

It made her wonder what the people whose voices she enjoyed on radio looked like. When she shut her eyes and attended only to Walter's voice she had found his success plausible. He prided himself that he could call up numbers in the book cold, just pick them at random, and realize over ten percent success. He represented a dozen companies, spent eight to ten hours a day on the phone, and earned over fifty thousand dollars a year.

Elaine had turned her head to look skeptically at him from the corner of her eye.

"I'll show you my tax form."

And he did. She took it with reluctance; it seemed to establish some kind of understanding between them. That was when she learned about his retarded sister Charlotte, who was cared for by a foster family.

"Cecil tells me to put her in a state hospital, let all the other taxpayers share the burden. What do you think of that?"

To tell the truth, Elaine thought it made sense. Half his income went to the support of his sister, but Elaine could hardly say so while Walter's face was contorted with contempt of Cecil, the man who helped him with his taxes.

"He's a wizard," Walter said.

"Because he said that?"

"No." And Walter showed her the cleverness with which Cecil kept Walter's taxable income low. Much depended on the claims made because of the cost of Charlotte's care. Didn't that involve other taxpayers as much as a state hospital would?

"It's not the same thing," Walter said indignantly.

"Why not?"

"It's just not."

If he argued that way on the phone, he'd never sell a thing. The conversation left Elaine feeling miserable. When Walter's income was adjusted for Charlotte's support, he netted less than she did, and that was not a promising economic basis for a life together.

"If I was married it would be different," he said when he called the next day.

"Different from being single?"

But he hadn't the slightest sense of humor, no matter the set jokes and hearty manner of his telephone persona. Of course he meant the amount of his taxable income. It seemed to characterize her relations with Walter that the implicit basis of their possible future was his income.

Once he called and disguised his voice and actually sold her subscriptions to two magazines she did not really want. After he identified himself, she told him to cancel the subscriptions, but in a minute he had convinced her all over again to take them. Much of his spiel had to do with the ridiculously small amounts she would pay, by credit card, for three months and then for two years...but she never clearly remembered what he had said. It did convince her that he would be a good provider.

A good provider. It all sounded like a bargain, a deal, a sale, rather than romance. That, she said to herself now, that is what she had been almost reconciled to until she met Gordon.

The first small difference was that Gordon would listen to her talk about her job as long as she cared to.

"You're kidding," he said when they were on the way to the Great Wall and she told him how she was transforming Captain Keegan's tirade about the Stacy Wilson investigation into a calm memo to the chief. She had babbled on and he listened, shaking his head, grinning his lopsided grin, all the way to the restaurant.

That afternoon when she had finished the memo, she did as she had promised and printed out a copy to show Gordon.

TWO

HE LIFTED HIS HAND as if her dry lips might leave a mark on his face—a brand, not lipstick—and watched her hurry up the courthouse steps. "Careful, Gordon," he warned himself, using the name he had told her was his. He had known a Gordon years ago in Red Wing, Minnesota, in what was officially called a school of correction but unofficially known as the reform school. No one had laughed when he said he wasn't Protestant. Gordon had black hair pushed straight back from a minimal forehead. Unbrushed, it fell on either side of his face, bracketing the expression of a boy trying unsuccessfully to understand what was going on. The association of the name with gourd was inevitable. With Elaine he was Gordonesque, taciturn, puzzled, pleasant. It was a switch being condescended to by her.

"Where'd you learn that?" she'd asked when he told her about alphabet language. She frowned at the napkin on which he had printed "F U N E X?" Did she think it was dirty?

"The response is, 'S, V F X.'" And he went through it all. "'F U N E M?' 'S, V F M,' 'OK. M N X.' Get it?"

"No."

"Ham an' eggs. M is ham, X is eggs..."

"That's dumb."

"You're right."

He never made that mistake again. He was Gordon and Gordons don't know jokes or puzzles. Letting her kiss him again when they parted was a bigger mistake.

He turned to walk away, starting around a pedestrian who stood in his way. The man moved into his path and again Gordon shifted. He had the absurd feeling he was dancing with this unprepossessing devil. But this wasn't an accidental encounter.

"Leave her alone."

Schoolyards, exercise yards, all the invisible hierarchies he'd had to learn, came to him, but then as quickly went. This guy was an annoyance at most.

"Her?"

With his head the guy indicated the courthouse steps, the movement a poppy pod waving on its stem. There were as many women ascending and descending the steps now as angels in the apocalypse. He let his incomprehension show.

"Elaine. The woman you had lunch with."

"Is that her name?"

His hands came out and pushed at Gordon. Gordon took him by the wrists, gently but firmly, and lowered the man's hands to his sides. He might have beat the shit out of him then and there.

"Leave her alone." This time through gritted teeth.

"All right."

He stepped back, surprised. "You mean it?"

"If you say so. Obviously she means more to you than she does to me."

Elaine had not mentioned another man and Gordon had just assumed there was none, which said a good deal of his estimate of her drawing power.

"I didn't mean to push you."

"She never mentioned you." An ambiguous remark. The poor devil didn't know whether to take comfort or insult from this. "Not that she would have, to a stranger."

"This isn't the only time. You've been with her a lot."

"Look, I don't know what people have been telling you." Of course he must have been following them. Gordon would have to think through their lunches to see how they appeared to others. But anyone would have seen her awkward kiss before she left him.

"Well, it's over in any case."

"Why should you just drop her because I..." It would have been difficult for him to characterize his actions.

"I'm leaving town."

HE WOULD TURN Walter's interference to advantage. Elaine could enjoy them more if their meetings had to be secret and furtive—women always did. In any case, he was far from through with her. It was amazing how many things she told him without being asked. She at least would never reconstruct their meetings as efforts on his part to pry from her details of the police work she was engaged in. Her offer to run off an extra copy of her report for Keegan was almost too good to be true.

The thought drove him into a saloon where he managed to distract the bartender from the ball game. The dumb shit had to put his back against the sink and crane his neck to follow the game. He should relocate the set where he could see it. Gordon pushed back the draft the man sailed at him.

"I'd like a full one."

The bartender looked in vain at the four men watching the game from barstools. "Sure." And he put a head on it that boiled over and ran down the glass, dampening the bar. It was an index of Gordon's preoccupation that he let the guy get away with it. The bartender wouldn't be the first one to be misled by the altar boy looks he had carried into manhood. Gordon decided to let him wait for his money.

Was it possible he'd been spotted and Elaine told to string him along to see what he wanted? The son of the notorious Stacey Wilson was not an ordinary suitor. Nor did he belong in Fox River. It was all too easy to imagine that someone had recognized him and told Elaine to find out what he was up to. He had three beers before he decided that couldn't be it. Elaine would have had to be an accomplished actress to carry off such a deception, and she was no actress at all. Her boyfriend's angry intervention told the same way, didn't it?

Maybe until you went behind those two. Someone could have spotted him and said nothing to Elaine, deciding to wait and see what developed, keeping an eye on them. It would be easy for a detective to monitor Elaine's actions.

While possible, this idea had nothing to support it. Not only would spotting him after all these years of keeping clear of his mother be close to impossible, the offer of the printout had to be Elaine's initiative. Besides, awkward as it might be to explain his interest in the secretary of the detective who had made the case against Stacey, he had done nothing wrong. He frowned. Mistakes, yes, but he had so far done nothing wrong.

THREE

"HONESTLY, the way that girl prays before St. Anthony, I'd think she was expecting," Marie Murkin said, her tone equivocal. Father Dowling had not noticed that Phil Keegan's secretary was all that regular a visitor to St. Hilary's.

"Maybe she has a vocation."

The corners of Marie's mouth dimpled impatiently. "More likely making a novena to catch a man."

"Good St. Anthony, get me a manthony as quick as you canthony?" That prayer was supposed to be addressed to St. Anne.

"And what's wrong with that?" The glint in Marie's eye suggested a readiness for theological disputation.

"Not a thing. Marriage is a vocation too."

He regretted saying it. Any pain the remark caused was unintended. Marriage was a delicate subject with Marie—her own, that is. Her husband had gone out to the store one day and never returned until years later, after she had been ensconced as housekeeper for years. The poor fellow had come back only to make a more definitive exit. The one title Marie could not abide was widow. The word suggested to her one who had been deprived of a lifelong companion and been left to fend for herself. "Grass widow," she had blurted out once, then begun to cry. Father Dowling after an awkward moment retreated to his study and a particularly full pipeload. He did the same thing now after uttering what in the context was a faux pas about the marriage vocation.

"She just got a raise," Phil Keegan said when Roger Dowling mentioned that Elaine McCorkle was often seen at her devotions in St. Hilary's Church.

"Maybe she's praying for a new job?" he teased.

"Maybe I am too. Roger, can you tell me how a man who is neither completely stupid nor totally dishonest can act like such an idiot."

The topic had ruined several ball games already, but Roger did not think his old friend's reaction to Chief Robertson's remark at a press conference—that he would never release the department's investigation into Stacey Wilson—was one with which he could fully sympathize. Predictably, Robertson's apparent obstinacy had become the heart of the conference and all the idiots from the press room landed on the chief with righteous anger. Did he deny the people's right to know? Did he think the papers of his department were privileged, on a par with the CIA? Swindel from the *Tribune* read portions from the Freedom of Information Act, which he apparently carried about with him like a talisman. It lent sanction to a generally fraudulent occupation, trying to trap public officials into making idiotic remarks which were then featured as the news of the day. Robertson had more than obliged them. Phil had suggested to the chief that he issue a statement saying he had misspoken. The chief's brow had lifted disdainfully at the suggestion.

The Fox River chief of detectives rose from his chair in Roger's study and flourished his cigar while he gave a pretty bad imitation of Robertson declaiming that he always said what he meant and meant what he said.

"So I suggested to the SOB that we at least provide a summary of the investigation. Roger, I'm proud of the way we nailed that woman. She married a wealthy man and killed him for his money and came within a hair of getting away with it. Robertson sounds as if we're hiding something and that plays into the hands both of the cretins from the press room and even more of Stacey Wilson's attorney. His appeal is based on the claim that there were procedural errors both during and before the trial. He knows better than simply to claim she's innocent."

Phil would never make a raconteur if he thought his summary of the Stacy Wilson case was adequate. It was a drama that Roger Dowling had followed with fascination. Seldom had he been so grateful for the way his friendship with Phil made him privy to the background of the case.

Marvin Wilson had married twice before taking Stacey to the altar in a garish little marriage chapel on the strip in Las Vegas. The setting seemed to suggest that he was making another losing bet in his life. His first wife, Lydia, had committed suicide, but that had been several years after the divorce. Her complaints to friends about Marvin's failure to keep her in the style the settlement required would have been matter for litigation if true, but Marvin's accountant was able to show he had been prompt and exact in fulfilling his financial obligations to his former wife. It would have been fanciful to hold him responsible for her death. Nonetheless, a suggestion of moral culpability clung to the man. His grandfather had made money and his father had added to it: they were the very model of the entrepreneur. Why then had Marvin's father, with the grandfather's enthusiastic collusion, raised the boy to be a moral idiot? He had attended several schools but graduated from none. Nor had he ever been gainfully employed. He spent a decade, more or less, imagining that he was a songwriter, influenced by an old Cary Grant/Alexis Smith movie about Cole Porter. Unlike his model, Marvin never put pen to paper and when he diddled at the piano, in search of a tune, he was rewarded only with phrases clearly stolen from popular songs. This velleity explained the three weeks Marvin had spent at Juilliard and the one course he had actually completed at Indiana University. When drunk at parties or in nightclubs Marvin could be counted on to commandeer the piano and empty the room.

Virginia, the second Mrs. Marvin Wilson, was still alive, though not under that name. Life with Marvin had made her serious. Roger Dowling had given Virginia instructions in the faith but had to tell her that her marriage with Marvin was an impediment to full participation in the sacraments. That brought back the agony he had felt as a member of the diocesan marriage tribunal. He had served on it for years after returning from Washington with his doctorate in canon law, daily confronted with the problems people created for themselves, problems all too often without any solution. How can adults really believe there is a solution to everything, some way to take life back to what it had been before a decision to marry? The hope was that they could be again what they had been then. Virginia, unlike most, profited from the realization that she could not undo what she had done. Marvin, of course, was under no such constraint. He divorced Virginia, his lawyer actually claiming alienation of affection for the time his wife had spent nursing AIDS patients with a group of Mother Teresa's sisters. Abandoned by Marvin, she now devoted herself entirely to that work. Perhaps she did not find the incurable nature of the illness of her patients so different from the common condition.

"You're lucky your name wasn't dragged into that case," Marie Murkin observed at the time.

"It would have been pretty good company."

"Marvin Wilson!"

"I was thinking of Mother Teresa."

And then had come Stacey Jones (it was only a stage name at first but she had legally adopted it), a leggy young lady who had wasted her life in Las Vegas, dancing, serving drinks, tending machines. She had dreamed of becoming a croupier but that was beyond her powers. No more could she deal cards. She had resigned herself to the role she was permitted to play, unwilling to leave the glitziness of a city built by gangsters and dedicated to draining off the honestly earned wages of the gullible who are airlifted into the desert. If the gambling equivalent to the alcoholic is someone who cannot stop at one, then Marvin Wilson was not a gambler. But he was gambler enough to be a welcome visitor to the city on the plains. His accountant provided him with one hundred thousand in cash for each junket and Marvin stayed until he had lost that amount. Of course he always lost, eventually, but there had been times when he had run his stake into millions, and then pressed onward to defeat. Thus he had met Stacey, who was predictably impressed by the amounts Marvin threw away but far more impressed by the unlikelihood that even he could succeed in throwing it all away. Clearly he was a not so young man in need of a wife who could bring a modicum of wordly wisdom to the marriage.

But within a year of the marriage Marvin Wilson was dead, in what might have been thought an accident if it had not come to light that Stacey had recently taken out an enormous policy on his life.

"Why was she so greedy?" Phil Keegan shook his head at the mystery of the human heart.

"She was the clear beneficiary of his will but she knew her claim to the family fortune would be contested. It was. The one thing she could be completely sure of was that insurance policy."

"Roger, it's funny how the price of a human life varies. Some people are killed for a thousand dollars."

And some victims of mugging for less. In the end, she had gotten nothing, not that it would have done her any good in prison where she was destined to spend the rest of her natural life. Odd how that phrase had hung on into an age when many doubted there was another life. A person cannot benefit from his crime. Once convicted of murdering Marvin Wilson, Stacey would not be paid by the insurance company. Inheriting Marvin's wealth was another matter, but relatives had emerged from the woodwork to contest the will and invoke like a moral absolute the principle that prevented Stacey from collecting on the insurance policy.

"Are you going to make a summary of the case for the press, Phil?"

"I already have. Elaine has it on her computer."

"I'd like to see it. To refresh my memory."

"I'll have her print you out a copy."

FOUR

A VIGILANT MARIE MURKIN had noticed that Elaine was a most infrequent presence at St. Hilary's, except of course on Sundays. As often as not, she fufilled her Sunday obligation by attending the late afternoon mass on Saturday, which was perfectly legitimate, although Marie did not approve of it. Get Mass out of the way, have the weekend for yourself, that was the idea. She had urged Father Dowling to preach about it.

"On Saturday nights?"

"That would be the best time."

"Marie, it may be difficult enough for people to come then. Why scold them for being no more Catholic than the Church?"

A delicate point, no doubt about it. Marie Murkin disapproved of the general easing of discipline that had been going on in the Church. No fast and abstinence anymore, even during Lent, not really.

"We get good turnouts for the Stations of the Cross," Father Dowling said.

Her complaints could turn him into a Pollyanna of optimism. It would have sounded like criticism telling him what it had once been like on Friday evening during Lent. The church had been packed! Not only did people go to Sunday Mass on Sunday, they had to fast from midnight before receiving Holy Communion. Now people got up, had a good breakfast, then went off to Mass and received communion. And confessions! Well, she didn't have to tell the pastor how they had fallen off. Oh, some things went on very much as before, like devotion to St. Anthony. It was Marie Murkin's experience that when people brought their problems to St. Anthony they were in real trouble. She approved of the sight of Elaine on her knees before the saint who never failed.

"You mean you spy on people when they pray in church?" Edith Hospers said sharply.

Marie had been so taken aback by that remark that she'd said an unforgivable thing. "Well, at least *you're* safe from my spying."

What an awful thing, to suggest that Edith never prayed. The words were hardly out of her mouth before Marie was begging Edith's pardon. They were on good terms when Marie left the school, now used to house the senior parishioners' activities, of which Edith had been the director since the center opened. But the chance of doing what Marie had gone over to the school to talk with Edith about was gone. Edith was sensitive enough about her husband, Earl, in the best of moods. And to think she had mentioned Elaine McCorkle only as a way into that topic.

Elaine worked for Captain Keegan, who had been instrumental in the conviction of Edith's husband. Even more interesting, Stacey Wilson was in the same prison as Earl. It had been Marie's hope that the conversation could get around to whatever Earl might have heard and seen of the notorious woman.

It wasn't that Marie couldn't imagine a woman killing her husband. She had wanted to do as much to hers for years and maybe she would have, given the opportunity. But her life with him had not been like Stacey's with Marvin Wilson. They hadn't lived together long enough and anyway the killing was cold-blooded. It was clear to Marie and millions of readers and viewers that Stacey had married Marvin for his money, then wanted the money without him, and hadn't wasted any time about trying to separate the two.

The truth was that Marie Murkin was fascinated by what the woman had done. She couldn't really imagine herself doing any such thing, not in a million years, but she could imagine wanting to and it was fascinating to read of someone who had. Why else did all those magazines at the checkout counter sell out week after week?

Now in her room, sipping tea, about to go to bed, her chagrin at the missed opportunity with Edith lessened, Marie closed her eyes and thought of those exciting days when Captain Keegan had been making the case against Stacey Wilson. Another memory came then and she opened her eyes as if to suffer the annoyance wide-eyed. Father Dowling, almost to the very end, had professed to doubt that Stacey was guilty.

"What did she have to gain?" he would ask.

"Money!"

"She already had money."

"No, her husband had money."

"He also had a habit of divorcing his wives and leaving them rather well off."

"She couldn't wait."

"Why?"

It was the Irish in him, of course; he had to be contrary, adopt a minority view and stick with it through thick and thin. The pastor had only stopped arguing for Stacey's innocence when Phil Keegan threatened to stop coming by the rectory.

"I get enough flak from that idiot Robertson."

"Does he think Stacey is innocent?"

"Innocent! He wanted me to pursue an anonymous tip that she had done away with his first wife too."

Well, having to go through all that again, typing up the report Phil Keegan had written, could very well have gotten on Elaine's nerves, but Marie Murkin had the notion that something else was bothering the secretary. Marie had already suggested that to the pastor. Did Father Dowling even know of Walter? Marie did. He came to the Saturday evening mass too, not exactly with Elaine, but usually they left together. Walter wasn't much, but then Elaine was no prize either and she surely wouldn't want to end up an old maid. The funny thing is that Marie would have thought Elaine was the hesitant one, for Walter seemed interested enough in her. So why the novena to St. Anthony?

Marie decided she would have a talk with Walter.

FIVE

WALTER HAD absolutely no right to ask her all these questions and Elaine made that perfectly clear. His scrawny throat rose out of a maroon turtleneck sweater Goodwill would have turned down and his great Adam's apple rode up and down it like the elevators at the courthouse. The thought that this creature had actually accosted Gordon and, and... Elaine had never been speechless before.

She was *darned* if she would ask Walter what had happened. Gordon's version was the only one that interested her. But Gordon didn't call. He didn't call and she had no idea how to reach him.

What had always before seemed the nicest and most romantic part of it—that Gordon had just materialized as if out of nowhere, that with him she lived only in the moment—now made her feel worse than foolish. She imagined trying to tell someone, not Walter, how she had met Gordon.

At the supermarket! He had gone through the line ahead of her and seemed absolutely helpless. And the things he had bought. Even the checkout girl laughed about it—snacks, sweet and salty, three kinds of soft drink, ice cream, juice, cereals—but he had turned to Elaine.

"I'm not used to this."

The obvious explanation was that his wife was away, but that wasn't it.

"I should have brought my mom with me."

His grin seemed to answer her question whether he was a mama's boy. He waited for her and they pushed their carts together into the parking lot.

"Well, this is my car," she said.

"These carts are neat."

"Where's your car?"

He didn't have one. In the circumstances she had to offer him a lift. He had insisted on getting out at the entrance of a new development that catered to singles. She could hardly have insisted that she wanted to see where he lived. Well, it turned out that he did not live at Carriage Estates, he never had.

"Gordon Jenkins?" Elaine had told the starch-voiced woman that she was inquiring on behalf of his mother.

She could not have made a mistake. Dear God, for weeks she had daydreamed of his apartment there, as if it were where they would begin their life together, as if... That they might anticipate the joys of matrimony was not of course something she could explicitly think, let alone imagine. That would have been to sin before the fact and if she were to sin in that way Elaine wanted the thing itself, not its anticipation. But her conscience had troubled her from the time she and Gordon had begun to see one another regularly.

What a way to put it! See one another. They had had a few lunches together, that was all. He was good-looking and deferential and he listened to her by the hour, but what more was there, after all? That impulsive kiss on the courthouse steps was emblazoned on her memory more gloriously than any of the other snapshots accumulated there. There had been a startled yet receptive look in his eyes as she leaned toward him, there had been the pleasantly abrasive sensation of whiskers and then his lips. If she had not turned and fled up the steps, what would have happened next?

The question tormented her more than those questions of conscience that had brought her to the feet of St. Anthony of Padua, a devotion she had taken on with her mother's milk. Mom had used St. Anthony as her intermediary in good times and in bad—there had been a little replica of the saint in her kitchen. It had gone with her to the rest home when her mind went, but by then not even that little brown-clad plaster figure with the baby Jesus in his arms could bring a flicker of recognition to her watery eyes. The statue had been buried with her. She had called good St. Anthony her passport to heaven. Was it only Elaine's imagination that the large figure in St. Hilary's was identical to her mother's miniature? Of course, the imagery was unimportant. How can we know what a long-ago saint actually looked like? Kneeling there, thinking thoughts like these, Elaine welcomed them as distractions. She was afraid to ask St. Anthony what she should do about Gordon.

What telling Walter might do to him was part of her worry, but surely God didn't want her to marry a man she could not bring herself to love when suddenly out of the blue there was Gordon. Wouldn't it be far crueler to marry someone she didn't love than to give him a few moments of pain now?

Oh, how she longed for that earlier anguish now that her problem was that Gordon seemed to have disappeared. In St. Hilary's Church, she knelt before the altar of her mother's favorite saint and could have wept aloud. The saint's face was long and thin with a curly brown beard the color of his religious habit. He gazed with large dark eyes at the baby he held, eyes of sadness rather than joy. If he had looked happy Elaine could not have gone on.

"Bring him back," she pleaded. "Let him at least phone."

She was convinced that her impulsive public kiss had driven him away, frightened or embarrassed him. He was so shy. That kiss wasn't like her at all, either, she was a private person. He must have seen that. But kissing him like that had been too much. She had robbed him of the initiative. Men needed the illusion that they were the leaders, not the led. Elaine knew all about it from the magazines she read. If she had known then what Walter had done she would have been tempted to call down the divine wrath on him.

After she rose from her knees, she became aware of a little woman in a coat sweater busying herself with the flowers at the next side altar. As if she had been waiting for Elaine to finish, she hurried to her and put a hand on her arm.

"Marie Murkin. I'm the housekeeper."

Elaine nodded.

"I'll keep your intentions in my prayers."

"Thank you."

"St. Anthony never fails."

"That's what my mother always said."

"She's gone?"

"Yes."

They observed a moment's silence at this apparent acknowledgment of the limitations to what St. Anthony was able to do. Mrs. Murkin's hand had slid to Elaine's. She turned it over. Was she looking for a ring? Suddenly Elaine felt that her purpose in coming here was transparent to everyone. An overweight woman of thirty-two pleading for a husband. She pulled her hand free.

"St. Anthony never fails," the housekeeper repeated.

Elaine stopped visiting St. Hilary's, but even so, two days later, Gordon called. At work.

"It's the only number I have."

"Where have you been?"

"I guess that means you've noticed I haven't been around."

"Gordon, Walter told me he talked with you."

"Funny little guy with a long neck?"

"I don't know what he told you."

"Let's get together and I'll tell you."

She could have cried out with pleasure. "The Great Wall?"

"No." A pause. "Are you free tonight?"

Thoughts chased one another through her mind. Walter had spoiled the Great Wall for them forever. Would she have time to clean up her apartment before he came? Did he want dinner? She felt a little dizzy trying not to think of the possible ultimate outcome of the evening.

But that wasn't what he had in mind at all. He gave her very elaborate instructions, which, despite his telling her not to, she wrote down. She was so excited to hear from him that she never once thought how childish these precautions were. She was going to see Gordon again!

"You remember the Stacey Wilson report? I'll bring you a copy of that."

"Oh, good."

After she put down the phone, she turned back to her computer. The green screen looked like something she had never seen before in her life. The keyboard was a senseless jumble of letters and symbols. She closed her eyes and began to thank St. Anthony, but halfway through she began to ask another favor. She left it vague—it wouldn't do to ask a saint's collusion in anything naughty.

Elaine wanted far more than a stolen public kiss.

SIX

AT WATER TOWER PLACE, from the upper levels, Gordon followed her progress through the detailed instructions he had given her. He was not surprised that from time to time she consulted a sheet of paper she did not quite remove from her purse. She had the lonely cappuccino on the second level, went up the escalator to a specified boutique where she looked at the overpriced merchandise for precisely twelve minutes, then went all the way down and outside again before returning in five minutes to mount directly to Rizzoli's where he awaited her. He had had to find out how malleable she was.

The intervention of the man she identified as Walter served to advance his relations with Elaine rather than the reverse. It had been a slow process gaining her confidence; she was not the kind of woman he had spent much time with and he did not want to frighten her.

Funny how Stacey had disapproved of the interest he took in the fillies in Vegas, younger versions of herself, gorgeous, not as smart as they thought, doomed. They were whores and didn't know it, not yet. But then they all dreamed of coming out of it the way Stacey had. What a bonanza Marvin Wilson had been, the answer to all her not-so-maidenly dreams. It was pure fantasy. Impossibly rich aging playboy, married and divorced twice, climaxing a great night at the tables with a shouted proposal. Everyone rose and accompanied the happy couple to a marriage chapel where the deed was done, legally, lots of witnesses, the story in the newspapers of the nation the following day.

Gordon had read it while on a morning coffee break at the Minneapolis grain elevator where he was working, sitting in a small cinder block room through whose dusty window was visible the Dante's inferno beneath the graceful cylinders that were such distinctive features of the city's skyline. Once parole boards had urged him to pursue the course indicated by his test scores, but finally everyone accepted his unwillingness to go to school of any sort. At the grain elevator, he moved among the slapping leather belts that constantly shifted the grain around, from one elevator to the next, reducing the chance of combustion. Little bottles of oil mounted above the rollers kept them lubricated and Gordon replenished the bottles as needed. From time to time there was a screw-up and grain would spill onto the floor, and Gordon and others would shovel it back onto the moving belt.

MARV MARRIES SHOWGIRL. He looked around although he knew he was alone. He even thought of putting his breathing mask back on. No one knew he had a mother who worked in Vegas. This was by mutual agreement. It would have destroyed her image to have a son his age, even though she had been sixteen when he was born, and he sure as hell didn't want anyone taunting him about a mother like her. But the story astounded him.

If this was right, Stacey had hit big casino at last. Gordon's embarrassment slipped away as he read of the wealth of Marvin Wilson. For the first time in his life he was proud of his mother. When he pulled on his cap and lifted the mask to his mouth and went out among the slapping belts of grain faintly illuminated by wire-enclosed bulbs, the atmosphere full of dust, it was with a light heart. Stacey's ship had come in at last. And so had his.

Were his elaborate and absurd instructions to Elaine a kind of revenge for the paces Stacey had put him through when he finally got through to her on the phone?

"Tyrone!" It was the name she had given him, derived from her favorite actor. "Where are you?"

"Congratulations."

This put her off her stroke. "Thanks. Thank you very much."

He could sense the calculation in her voice when she went on. She did not have to tell him that her son was a secret from Marvin Wilson.

"It's been a long time, Stacey."

"Don't you dare say how long." She hated anything that could measure her age.

"Just call it too long."

"Tyrone, where are you right now?"

"I'm calling long distance."

"I can help you now, you know. Where can I send you something?"

Meaning, she wanted to keep him at a distance. Well, why not? He had no sentimental urge to see her again. The photographs in the newspaper summoned no pleasant childhood memories. But of course the papers had run publicity photos from her agency. The girl with the wide plastic smile, glittering eyes, and offered bosom was a cliché, no one in particular. How could she be his mother? She wired him five thousand and the tacit understanding was that this would go on.

"How should I send it?" she'd asked.

"You said wire."

"I meant what name?"

"Tyrone Pajakowski."

There was a long pause on the line. He had never changed his name to Jones but retained that of the sailor on liberty who had knocked up Stacey on a single attempt, if she was to be believed. But then he had to believe her that the swabbie's name was Pajakowski.

"I'll wire it now."

And she did. He had never known the normal anxieties of life, where the next meal was coming from, whether he would have a roof over his head, what tomorrow would bring. Institutions had provided him with total security and he had always felt vaguely uneasy in leaving them. Was it the certainty that he would be back that made freedom tolerable? Nothing on the outside could compare with a cushy job in the laundry, say, or hours during which to read his way through the prison library. He had never liked television. It was like letting the outside world disturb his peace. Books were different. Books were in his head.

Five thousand every two months, that was what it came to. Tyrone had received a total of twenty-five thousand when it stopped with the death of Marvin Wilson.

Wilson had taken Stacey to the family estate on the Fox River situated on a rise of land that gave a fine view of the river. But it was Lake Michigan that drew the Wilsons. They had always kept boats and Marvin shared the passion of his father and grandfather for Great Lake yachting. Stacey almost never went with him, preferring to ride her tame mare on the farm's well-trodden paths. She hated water. The huge lake had a wicked look, dark, cold, extending like rippling metal toward the horizon.

Marvin had gone out alone in an eighteen-footer in marginal weather. His boat drifted ashore two days later. He lay in its bottom in half a foot of water, with a nasty head wound that had stopped bleeding when his heart stopped pumping. The initial judgment was that he had been felled by the boom in a sudden shift of wind. That this could happen to an experienced sailor was attributed to the violence of the wind. The former Las Vegas showgirl was suddenly the heiress to a fortune.

Tyrone waited a decent length of time—it would have been unseemly to present himself too soon. That the new widow had a son was not known and the presence of a young man immediately after her loss might attract publicity he would have found as unwelcome as she. For several weeks the scandal magazines had a holiday with the story of the showgirl's inheritance. Old friends who had kept quiet at the time of the marriage now spoke to reporters and were no match for their questions.

A witness appeared who was certain he had seen Mrs. Wilson with her husband on the fateful day as they prepared the boat to go out. Her absence from the farm was then established; she had not been seen at home since her husband sailed into a stormy Lake Michigan. Had she been aboard, below? Had his head wound been an accident or caused by her? Had she ridden out the storm with the dead body of her husband and then scrambled free when it reached shore? There was no doubt that she had been at the Fox River farm to receive the grim news of his death.

Once started, the speculation did not stop and Tyrone followed it with fascination, trying to calculate what it meant for him. It was not simply the junk journalists of the supermarket scandal sheets who pursued it but the mainline media as well. It was a period when there was little news and scandals real and imagined held unusual attractions. The story of the former showgirl who had ended up with piles of respectable cash was turned into a cold-blooded plot to kill her husband before he tired of her and thus be assured of getting everything and not merely what a divorce might bring. It was amusing when the scion of a staid midwestern family married a Stacey Jones. Titillation was assured when such a woman inherited the whole kaboodle. But righteous anger began at the thought that she had killed her husband to attain this result. Here was greed and the public would not stand for it. The newspapers told them so. Demands for an investigation multiplied.

Tyrone thought Stacey was lucky that the investigation fell within the jurisdiction of the Fox River police. But he reckoned without the tenacity of Philip Keegan, who slowly built a case a prosecutor was able to convince the jury with. Six months after she had become a wealthy woman, Stacey Wilson was in prison, penniless, a ward of the state for life. It was time for Tyrone to visit his mother.

Time, too, to look into the account she'd opened in Switzerland and to which she had transferred large amounts of cash. She said she couldn't remember the account number, but it was written on a card he could find in her purse.

"The one I had with me when they arrested me."

"Where is it?"

"If it isn't at home, the police must still have it. It's alligator with silver snaps in the shape of alligator heads."

It wasn't at the farm in Fox River. It wasn't in the Chicago pied-à-terre near the Water Tower. The police must have retained it.

The purse contained his matrimony.

Stacey wrinkled her nose. "Your what?"

"I can't say patrimony. What did Pajakowski ever give me?"

"Once," she said musingly. "Just once. A quickie. And here you are."

"It makes you think," he said.

"It makes me laugh."

"Thanks."

"This is my last chance to screw the bastards. Get that money, Ty. I want you to have it." Her face twisted in sudden anguish. "I didn't do it, Tyrone. I swear to God I didn't kill him."

"I read the papers."

"Get out of here."

But he pressed his hand against hers before leaving.

It had taken him a while to figure out how to claim his inheritance, but now Elaine, moving through the book tables of Rizzoli's toward him, a smile of diffident expectation on her face, was the solution. He was sure of it.

SEVEN

ROGER DOWLING, reading the summary of the Wilson case Phil Keegan had provided him, was struck even more foricibly than he had been at the time of the trial by the fragile basis on which the prosecution had rested.

First had been the testimony of Billy Wheaton, who claimed to have seen Stacey on the eighteen-footer with her husband just before it set sail. Two other witnesses had watched the boat head out into the lake, but only Marvin had been visible. The conclusion, if Billy was right, was that Stacey was below.

But that begged the question of her being aboard at all. Not even Billy Wheaton had been willing to say he actually saw her on the boat after it set sail or had any way of knowing she was aboard.

So the prosecution had moved to the fact that the whereabouts of Stacey Wilson during the relevant days when the boat had been on the lake were unknown. If there was any way she could have established an alibi the case would have crumbled. Her claim to have spent the time in her room ailing, seeing no one, went unsupported by the staff. They did, however, offer vivid accounts of the quarrels between Marvin and his new wife. The defense elicited the fact that Marvin had quarreled similarly with all his wives but this went for naught. He had survived his quarrels with them.

The fact that clothing of hers had been found on the *Lucky Tyke* was given great significance by the prosecution, but clothing of hers had been found in the lockers of the two other Wilson boats as well.

The pastor of St. Hilary's could not believe that such a prosecution had succeeded, but it had. And worse, it was one of Phil Keegan's boasts that it was the work of his department that had made it all possible. His dispute with Robertson was a dispute between two versions of triumphalism. Thus it was that Roger Dowling broached the subject with some caution. They were lunching after the pastor's noon mass, which Phil had attended.

"To get a free lunch," Marie said, but she said it with affection and to Phil. She loved cooking for a man who relished his food as obviously as Phil did.

"I've been reading your summary of the Wilson case, Phil."

"Oh, it's Elaine McCorkle's more than mine. She had to put it into English and remove all the French."

"And do a little research as well?"

"It's all at her disposal, Roger. On the computer. Everything's on the godforsaken computer now."

"A critic would call it a flimsy case."

"Flimsy?"

"Let me be the devil's advocate, Phil."

"When aren't you?" Phil nodded at Marie who in sign language was asking if he wanted another beer.

"What does it matter? She's where she belongs, behind bars."

Marie nodded in vigorous agreement, then poured his glass full.

"If she's guilty."

"She was tried and convicted."

"And she has appealed the verdict."

"Roger, there's no way the appeal won't be turned down."

Billy Wheaton had died in the meantime, a derelict's death, gone to God in a drunken stupor, the eyes that claimed to have seen Stacey Wilson on the *Lucky Tyke* with her husband blind to the things of this world now.

"Alive or dead, Billy Wheaton's testimony was a slender reed, Phil."

"Where was she all that time, Roger? That's the question. All she had to do was prove she was somewhere else. Instead she told a lie so obvious that not even the employees could back her up."

"Doesn't that puzzle you?"

"That someone tells a wild story when caught? No, Roger, it doesn't. Anything else would surprise me. How many people really want to believe they've done something wrong? Marie, go to the kitchen, I want to tell a story."

Marie of course pulled out a chair and sat at the table while Phil told the story of a man who was driving with his mistress beside him and stopped at a traffic light. His wife pulled up next to him. He looked at her and she loooked at him and he cried out, "It's not me, Charlotte. I swear to God it's not me."

Marie harrumphed rather than laughed, tucked in her chin and glared at Phil, then disappeared into the kitchen.

"You get my point, Roger."

"Never tell stories to a housekeeper?"

"Aw, you're as bad as she is."

Phil went back to work and Roger Dowling went to his study and read for a time in the Third Part of the *Summa theologiae,* but after a single article he closed the book and lit his pipe. Until he remarked on it just now to Phil, had he fully realized that Stacey Wilson must have known how transparently false her alibi was? She could not have thought for an instant it would hold up, and that must mean she expected it to fall apart. The cook and gardener were questioned separately and both expressed surprise at the claim that Mrs. Wilson was home during the days Mr. Wilson had been away.

Father Dowling took up the printout of the synopsis Phil had given him. Some synopsis. It ran to 150 pages single spaced. But it did not contain the information he sought.

Perhaps a report of twice that length would not, perhaps no report that could now be written.

If Stacey was not on the boat and not at home she was somewhere, and she had risked prosecution and lifelong imprisonment to keep it secret. Why? Somewhere—and with someone? But for whom would she give up her freedom? The deed suggested a heroism difficult to associate with the woman whose life had been described in such lurid detail before and during the trial.

He called Phil's office and when Elaine answered put the question to her.

"Was Stacey Jones ever married before her marriage to Wilson?"

"Who is this?"

"I'm sorry. This is Roger Dowling. I've been reading your report on the Wilson case with great interest. It brings it all back so vividly."

"Why thank you."

"Was Jones her married name?"

"Apparently not. She changed her name to Jones as a professional matter. There was no Mr. Jones."

"What was her name before that?"

"I'd have to look it up." Her tone told heavily against the likelihood of her doing so.

"Did Stacey have any family?"

"I wondered about that too."

"Did you?"

"Because no one showed up to support her. No one. That was sad, even given what she'd done. But would relatives have come forward when she was accused of such a crime? If she has a family they've disowned her."

"Did you wonder about the story she told of where she was when her husband was out in that storm?"

"When people are caught they'll say anything."

Well, that seemed to be the consensus of the Fox River police, at any rate. Thinking about it, Roger Dowling had to admit that it rang true. How often had he listened to people explain what they had done in such a way that they themselves were not responsible?

And then Elaine abruptly changed the subject.

"Father, this isn't the time, but I'd like to discuss something with you."

"Of course."

"Tomorrow?"

Hadn't Marie mentioned seeing Elaine at St. Hilary's? "I say Mass at noon. Before or after is fine with me."

"Not at the rectory."

"I'll be in the sacristy afterward."

"I'll come there."

She hung up, leaving the pastor of St. Hilary's staring perplexed at the telephone.

"IT'S THE HOUSEKEEPER," Elaine said the following day. She was waiting for him in the sacristy when he finished Mass.

"Marie?"

"Father, she had the nerve to tell Walter I've been here praying that he'd propose and of course he did!"

Roger Dowling removed chasuble and alb deliberately, trying to make sense of this.

"Who's Walter?"

"Walter Nickles. It doesn't matter. She had no right."

"Tell me exactly what happened." Any thought of inviting her to lunch with him where she would confront the object of her wrath was clearly out of the question.

Elaine had indeed been visiting St. Hilary's and she had indeed been making a series of novenas to St. Anthony of Padua but she did not see what business that was of Marie Murkin's. Father Dowling could scarcely disagree.

"How she even knew about Walter is beyond me."

"Marie takes a motherly interest in all members of the parish," he said lamely.

Marie had put together what she clearly regarded as two and two and decided to do St. Anthony's work for him. So she had contacted the supposed object of Elaine's affections and urged him to make his move. He had, to the great consternation of Elaine McCorkle.

"I take it you and Walter aren't going together."

"Not in that way."

"I understand."

But did he? What he understood was that Marie had done something unforgivable. The question was how to punish her. There seemed only one way.

"Come to lunch, Elaine. We can discuss this more conveniently there."

"But won't she be there?"

"Only to wait upon us, Elaine. Only to wait upon us."

EIGHT

TUTTLE REMEMBERED the Wilson investigation and trial in all its details. His was a mind made for case law. Whatever difficulties he had had getting through law school, something he had done thanks to the financial and moral support of his late father, now immortalized in the name of the firm, Tuttle & Tuttle, memorizing cases had not been among them.

"Billy Wheaton's drunken testimony," he said to Peanuts Pianone, who was carefully removing from a plastic container the last of the fried rice. "It's all right here." 'Here' was the audiocassette that Tuttle flourished. "If I had a machine I'd play it for you."

"I've heard it."

Tuttle had cornered Wheaton in a Waukegan bar and bought him drinks while he interviewed him. His intention had been to cross up the drunken bastard so he could sell the tape to Stacey Wilson's lawyers and cut himself in on the loot they must be earning. But who would pay if they lost? No wonder they were appealing. It was either that or chalk up months of high-cost effort to experience. But the best Tuttle had got out of Billy was that the figure in the boat might not have been Stacey Wilson.

"It might not have been a woman. Hell, Tuttle, it could have been a flying horse. It could have been lots of things. Only it was her."

Tuttle considered editing the tape but where would he be if Billy Wheaton blew the whistle on him? Now that Billy was dead that danger was passed. Tuttle was excited and the torpor of his lunch companion did not faze him.

They were in Tuttle's office, a cluttered place, and the attorney wore his tweed hat, his thinking hat, and was so absorbed he had hardly touched his sweet and sour pork.

"You going to eat that, Tuttle?"

"Go ahead." He pushed the plastic tray toward Peanuts, who quickly took possession of it.

How could he eat now? This was like being in love.

"Peanuts, all my life I've had my eye out for what the French call the grand coop."

"The grand coop."

"Maybe it's coupé."

"The grand coop." Peanuts snickered. "It sounds like Joliet." Tuttle gazed at him benignly. Peanuts's reaction did not offend him. He would have been worried if Peanuts understood. Peanuts was the dim-wit of a family that had been operating in Fox River without any convictions for two generations and had decided to put Peanuts on the police force when it became clear he was not shrewd enough for any of the family businesses. Peanuts was tolerated on the force as Tuttle was tolerated, just barely, by his profession, yet the lawyer looked with condescension on the lowly lawman. And with affection. There were chilling moments when he realized that Peanuts might be the only real friend he had, and he wasn't sure he could count on Peanuts in the crunch.

None of it mattered now—his ambiguous career, the disregard in which he was generally held (he tried so few cases he was seldom in contempt of court, but ever in the bar's contempt), the sense of failure in fulfilling his father's self-sacrificing trust. It all paled before the certainty that success would be his after all. No need to spell it out for Peanuts. Better not to speak of it to anyone. He pushed back from his desk, stood, took off his hat and put it on again.

"Up and at 'em, Peanuts. Got to get to work."

"Yeah?"

"You got a squad car at your disposal?"

"Out back."

"Come along then. You may learn something."

"I'll wait for you."

If he dared drive the squad car himself, Tuttle would have agreed. "I wouldn't, Peanuts." He glanced at his watch. "They should be here by now."

"Who?"

Tuttle considered what would most likely chase from Peanuts's mind the thought of napping in the chair he sat in for the rest of the afternoon.

"The plasterers. Of course you could help them drape their cloths before they take down that ceiling. I don't want them to ruin my law books."

"I'll come with you."

"I'd feel safer if you'd supervise..."

But Peanuts was already on his way out the door. Tuttle followed, whistling silently.

He had Peanuts stop at his apartment where he picked up the little battery-operated recorder he had used in deposing Billy Wheaton. That is what he'd told the poor lush he was doing, though he had no status in the case. Billy had been unsure whether he was with the prosecution or the defense or maybe another lawman. The other two tapes were still in the torn-open plastic package from which he had taken the cassette on which Billy Wheaton had sung his swan song. Tuttle stuffed them into his pocket and put the recorder in his briefcase. He closed his eyes as he buckled down the straps. His father had given him that briefcase when he was in his fifth year of law school. He made a silent promise to the paternal parent. When he opened his eyes, they were damp. He hurried down to the squad car.

"Where to?" Peanuts asked.

"The Wilson farm."

"You serious?"

"Never more so."

Peanuts, faithful Tonto, put the car more or less in gear and moved away from the curb to a metallic complaint from beneath the hood. But soon they were under way.

Tuttle put the Billy Wheaton tape on and listened to a minute or two of it before turning off the machine.

He wasn't sure how much life the batteries had. The sound of Billy's slurred voice shook his confidence in his scheme, but only momentarily. What he wanted was a chorus of voices.

The entrance to the farm loomed unexpectedly after they came over a rise in the road, and Peanuts nearly rolled the car when Tuttle yelled "Turn!" The car righted and Tuttle pushed his hat back off his eyes, his heart pounding. If Peanuts had turned in the right direction he might have collided with one of the brick columns that bracketed the road to the farm. As it was, they were pointing away from it, the nose of the squad car dipping into the ravine like a horse led to water.

"Back up."

"The motor died."

As they sat there the car dipped forward more definitely. Tuttle opened his door and jumped out. This had the unexpected effect of stopping the car's descent. Tuttle bent over and looked in at Peanuts. "I thought that would do it. Start her up."

Their arrival had been observed by the man on the lawn tractor who was methodically moving back and forth across the enormous stretch of grass that drew the eye up the hill to where the house was visible within its protective stand of trees. Halfway up the graveled road, Tuttle told Peanuts to stop. The man on the tractor kept on mowing.

"This thing got a siren?"

For answer, Peanuts sent its insistent wail over hill and dale. He sent the gumball on the top in motion too. This got the mower's attention. Tuttle activated the voice amplifier.

"Now hear this. We're looking for Willis McNaughton. McNaughton. Willis. We are looking for..."

The man on the mower came toward them at a great clip, waving one arm, steering erratically with the other, as if to stop Tuttle from announcing to the world that the police had come for him. He hustled them into the house.

McNaughton's face had the smoothness of scar tissue, which gave the effect of a mask; eyes like black aggies looked fixedly at Tuttle. His wife's eyes were for the recording machine on the table between them. Peanuts took up his position by the door of the kitchen in which Tuttle had set up shop. Good man. He gave this the air of an official proceeding.

"I thought it was all over," Willis said.

"They've appraised the place God knows how many times," said his wife.

"Mrs. Wilson's lawyers have filed an appeal. That is of course their right. I want fresh statements from the two of you..."

"Shouldn't we talk to Griese, Will?" She turned to Tuttle. "He's our lawyer."

"Counsel isn't present at depositions," Tuttle said briskly.

"You represent her?" McNaughton asked.

Tuttle laughed in what he meant to be a contagious way, looking to Peanuts to chime in. But he laughed alone.

"The law is on no one's side," he said unctuously. "What I want is brief statements about the two and a half days when Marvin Wilson was absent from this house and, as we know, was adrift on Lake Michigan, lying dead in his schooner, *Lucky Tyke.*"

"We were here," McNaughton said.

"Precisely. And that is why I am here. Did you see Mrs. Wilson during the period of Mr. Wilson's absence from the house?"

"She wasn't here." Mrs. McNaughton endorsed her husband's statement, nodding so vigorously her great breasts were set in motion.

"When did she leave?"

"She wasn't here."

"I understand that. When did you last see her? I mean, when was the last time you remember seeing her before the discovery of Mr. Wilson's body."

McNaughton put a hand on his wife's shoulder. "We thought she was with him."

"Why?"

"Isn't that what the trial proved?"

"Why would she kill him?"

Mrs. McNaughton's face firmed and she sat straighter in her chair. "He was no angel but she was another."

"They were both unfaithful?"

McNaughton intervened. "That's not a thing we can know," he said, then added as if in honor of the occasion, "of our own knowledge."

Tuttle continued this for ten minutes, going round in circles, hoping an opening would show itself, but his batteries gave out and, while he did not let on and made a show of turning off the machine, he brought the session to a close with the feeling that he had not added much of value to the Billy Wheaton tape. That remained his passport to a better life.

They could hear the radio as they went out to the car. Peanuts increased his speed slightly and answered the call with the indolence of one sure of his job.

"Pianone, where the hell are you?"

"Pianone here."

"Where the hell is here?"

Tuttle shook his head.

"East of town. I followed what I thought was a stolen vehicle."

"You get back here or you'll be driving one."

"What's up?" Peanuts asked blandly.

But the dispatcher had signed off.

NINE

ELAINE HAD NEVER BEEN so confused in her life. Gordon had revealed himself to be Tyrone Pajakowski. He told her this while holding both her hands in his and looking her straight in the eye.

"I lied to you and I'm sorry. If you got up and walked out of my life right now I wouldn't blame you a bit."

Out of his life? Did that mean she was in it? The name Tyrone Pajakowski meant nothing to her—why would he have wanted to conceal it from her? One question gave way to another but she did not free her hands from his. She felt that he had posed a problem they must solve together.

"Tyrone." She tried the name, liking it. "I prefer it to Gordon."

He laughed. "So do I. I was beginning to act like Gordon."

There was something different about him now, his manner, even his speech. He no longer seemed just a good-looking shy man only slightly younger than herself who needed looking after.

"Why did you use that name?"

"Don't you know?"

He searched her face for the answer to his question but Elaine had no idea what he was referring to.

"It's not in your report but that doesn't mean the police didn't turn it up."

"What report?"

"The Wilson case."

"But what has that got to do with you?"

"Elaine, remember when we met. It was when you told me where you worked that I decided to call myself Gordon. Whenever you talked of your work I wanted to stop you. It was too painful. And then you offered me your report. How could I refuse?"

Lots of people had been moved in lots of ways by the Wilson case, Elaine understood that. She herself had vacillated between sympathy for Stacey and the chilling hope that the woman would get what was coming to her. Of course, in the department she could not express any doubt that Stacey should be convicted and sentenced to life. "We're not in the mercy business," Captain Keegan had said more than once. "We'll leave that to Father Dowling. And the courts," he added after a moment, glowering around the room at whatever investigative team was assembled before him. "Our Bible stops with the Old Testament." Elaine had jotted that down so many times you'd think she'd know what he meant, but she didn't, not really, though she understood it would have been fatal to express any sympathy with Stacey Wilson around Captain Keegan.

"She was guilty, Gor—Tyrone. It will take me a while to get used to that. What if I told you now my name was really Ann or Barbara?"

He laughed. "I'd call you sweetie until I got used to it." He squeezed her hands and leaned toward her. Elaine didn't move, wanting it to be clear this time who was kissing whom. Her eyes closed and light as a moth his lips came and went on hers.

"Don't waste your sympathy on Stacey Wilson. Have you read the report?"

"Of course."

"It's pretty open and shut."

"Elaine, it's not her guilt that bothers me."

"What then."

He let go of her hands now, laying his flat on the marble top of the little pizzeria table. His face remained inches from hers.

"I think she's my mother."

He was serious, there seemed no doubt of that. Elaine waited for some sign that it was a joke but after a moment she knew he meant it. Her first reaction was that he was crazy, like one of the poor souls who show up during an investigation to confess and know only what they have read in the newspaper. Whatever they were guilty of it was not the crime to which they confessed. Was that how Tyrone came to think Stacey Wilson was his mother?

"She couldn't have a son your age."

"I'm twenty-nine. She's forty-five, going on forty-six."

"Forty-two."

"She's lying. That's a lady's prerogative."

"She'd lie about you too," Elaine said, grasping at the thought. She was filled with depression by this fantasty of Tyrone's.

"Not if I had proof."

"What kind of proof?" Was he thinking of a blood test? Elaine put her hands on his, still flat on the table, and she could have cried, she felt so sorry for him.

"Find out where she was twenty-nine years ago. What she was doing."

"But how?"

"Ask her."

They left the pizzeria, took the escalator down and walked up Michigan Avenue while he told her of the memories that had been triggered when he first saw the photo of Stacey in the paper, when she married Wilson. He wanted to look her up then, but had neither the time nor the money. What was the rush? Now he knew where she was.

"You probably wonder why I didn't go to her during the trial, when she could have used some support. Everyone was against her then."

Elaine looked at him, waiting for the answer.

"I thought it would add to her troubles, not lighten them. More guilt. She didn't need that then. Elaine, I didn't think she'd be convicted."

It seemed better not to say anything.

"Before I go see her I want you to do something for me."

"What?"

At her expression of alarm he stopped and smiled, shaking his head. Then he slipped his arm around her waist and they continued walking. Most pedestrians were going in the opposite direction, but they opened and closed around them and Elaine took this as deference to a young couple in love. There was no need to pretend otherwise now. She was in love with him, Gordon or Tyrone or Batman, she didn't care what he called himself. In Rizzoli's she had felt his strength but now it was his vulnerability that drew her. It broke her heart to think of someone twenty-nine years old in search of a mother he had never really known.

"What can I do, Tyrone?"

His idea was as fantastic as the thought that he was the son of Stacey Wilson. He was convinced that there would be some clue in her purse. It had figured in the trial as an indication of the gifts her husband had lavished on her. Tyrone was certain she would have carried around some proof of their relationship—a picture, a birth certificate, something. He seemed certain the purse was still in the custody of the police. Had that been in her synopsis? She couldn't remember.

"I'll look."

"I wish I could be with you."

He pressed against her as they walked, his arm firm around her waist. She didn't care if he was a little nutty.

"We'll see," she said.

TEN

"SOMEONE TO SEE YOU, Father." Marie scooted across the study to a window and raised it and began to make sweeping gestures with her arms.

"Something the matter?"

"You could smoke hams in here."

"Then hang around."

"Oh, ha ha. He's in the front parlor."

This was a transformed Marie. After she had served luncheon to Elaine McCorkle, the pastor gave her a scolding, instructing her that until she had been ordained and/or had been given the care of the souls of this parish she was to leave such matters in his own doubtless incompetent hands. Ever since, Marie had been a chastened woman. She went about her work silently, she kept her eyes lowered, she responded with deference and alacrity to Father Dowling's wishes: she was paying him back. He had been seeking some honorable way to restore things to their even tenor when Marie bounded into his study as if she had the world on a string.

Her all too audible humming followed him down the hall.

The visitor stood just inside the door of the parlor, as if he had just scooted back to where Marie had put him.

"Father Dowling," the pastor said and extended his hand. The man dropped back and began to crumple. The priest hurried to his assistance.

"Are you all right?"

"I thought you were going to bless me."

The man put Father Dowling in mind of the folding rulers carpenters carried. Apparently he had been about to kneel. Now he stood upright.

"I'm not Catholic."

"Well, I found out you're not a Shaker either."

His laugh was surprisingly hearty. "I suppose you don't bless non-Catholics."

"Only for a fee."

Again the laugh. It was reassuring, given the man's skeletal aspect. He couldn't weigh more than 140 pounds—there wasn't a spare pound on him, and his head seemed small, perhaps because of the length of his neck.

"Walter Nickles, Father Dowling." He collapsed into a chair without invitation and his face contorted in grief. "I really should have spoken to the woman who let me in. Marie Murkin, isn't she?"

"You've heard of her?"

"I owe her a lot. She brought things to a head. I suppose she told you about it. Elaine doesn't love me. There's someone else."

So this was the man Marie had thought Phil's secretary was praying to St. Anthony about.

"Marie is worth her weight in pyrites."

"I couldn't agree more." The man could use a neck brace with a neck that thin. He pointed to some magazines on the corner table. "I'd hate to be stuck here for long with only that stuff to read."

"I try not to keep people waiting."

"I suppose you saw the article about the Trappists in the recent issue of *Country Gentleman.*"

"No, I didn't."

"I'll send you a copy. How about newsmagazines? Care to lengthen your subscription? There are a number of premiums now available."

"What do you do for a living?"

"Guess."

"Do you go from door to door?"

The head swayed negatively. "I work entirely by telephone. Not without success. I would starve going door to door but I do extremely well on the phone."

Roger Dowling became aware of the man's voice as he said this and found the claim credible.

"That is what I shall be leaving behind."

"But I thought you said Elaine..."

His hand, when he lifted it, looked as if it would span an ocatave and a half. "I have a vocation, Father Dowling I'm sure of it. I want to become a Trappist."

"But you're not a Catholic."

"I suppose that comes first."

"Walter, there are several things one should not do on the rebound—marry another woman or enter a religious order. Any vocation director would advise you to delay."

"The world has lost its taste for me, Father. Have you ever eaten grits? No? Absolutely without taste. Southerners claim to love them. Well, I suppose I could acquire a taste for the tasteless world. But I prefer to say goodbye to it all."

"A vacation may be all you really need."

"Good idea. I thought I'd spend a week in a monastery. Could you run interference for me?"

Roger Dowling offered to talk with him about it in a week's time. By then his romantic notion of burying himself in the cloister should have subsided. If not, he would arrange for Walter to spend a few days in a monastic retreat house. Hankerings after asceticism and isolation seldom survived such a visit.

When he rose to go, Walter stuck out his hand.

"Would you like a blessing?"

His grin transformed him. Father Dowling traced the sign of the cross over Walter, who insisted on getting down on one knee. The priest then walked his visitor out to his car. Between the rectory and the church Walter stopped and looked around. He inhaled deeply and looked down on the pastor with a beatific smile.

"This is what I want. Peace. Solitude."

Marie Murkin stood in the kitchen door when he returned, an expectant expression on her face.

"Wedding bells?"

"More like mission bells. He wants to enter the monastery."

She could not decide whether or not to take him seriously. She spun on her heel and stomped into her kitchen. As he passed through, Roger Dowling tried in vain to hum the maudlin tune made popular by Bobby Vale several decades earlier.

ELEVEN

THE NIGHT BEFORE on "Larry King" some Jesuit had been cussing out the church for not ordaining women as well as for not permitting priests to marry and Phil Keegan, a widower for half a dozen years but still in possession of realistic memories of his marriage, wondered what the guy imagined married life was like. The Jesuit wore a business suit and a yellow tie. He looked and sounded like that yo-yo McLaughlin. Keegan went to bed in a rage.

Throughout the night, sleeping and waking, he debated the matter of a married priesthood. On his way to work, he decided to put the question to Roger Dowling. He called him first thing.

"Is this a proposal, Phil? Whom are you representing?"

"I'm serious, Roger. Would you want a wife?"

"You're asking a man who spends a good deal of his day with Marie Murkin."

"Hey, she's an angel compared to some women."

"I'll tell her you said so."

"I'll tell her myself."

"Go ahead. She's probably listening in."

A little gasp on the line told Phil this was true. "I take back what I said about you, Marie."

"And what was that?"

"Answer me a question, Marie. You still on, Roger?"

"He hung up," Marie said.

"Good. Then you can tell the truth for a change. Do you think priests ought to be married?"

He settled back and listened while Marie rattled off sound doctrine on the subject. She had nothing against marriage, she insisted—who did?—but the life of a priest makes special demands, he has to regard everyone as his family, with an equal claim on him.

"How about housekeepers?" Roger was apparently still on the line. "Should they be married? I think Phil may have an important question to put to you, Marie."

Phil imagined three phones hanging up simultaneously. Then Elaine came in.

"Captain Keegan?"

"What is it, Elaine?"

"What happens to the evidence presented at a trial. I mean afterward."

"My God! Not you too."

Elaine stepped back as if he had struck her. What the hell. He was getting too damned touchy when he resented his own secretary taking an interest in the work of the department.

"That depends on the case, Elaine."

She was mollified by his change of manner. "It was doing the report on the Wilson case that made me wonder."

"Did I tell you that was a very good report? I've received several compliments which I now pass on to you."

"What happened to Stacey Wilson's purse? Alligator skin, with silver snaps like the jaws of an alligator."

Leave it to a woman to remember a thing like that. "Have you checked with the prosecutor?"

"He says they sent everything back to us."

"So there are you."

"Where is it kept?"

Her question appealed to the teacher in him. Imagine being here as many years as Elaine had been and not knowing about the Black Museum. Every time he said the phrase, Phil dropped his voice into Orson Welles register, he couldn't help it, but of course Elaine would not have heard that old radio program.

"It's time you saw it. Anything on right now?"

"Your calendar is clear."

"Have someone cover for you."

They took the elevator to the basement and went through a heating tunnel to a building across the street from the courthouse, emerging into the furnace room. The door out of there was not flush with the floor and Elaine had to lift her foot over the sill. Captain Keegan shut the steel door of the furnace room behind them. They now stood in a large, low-ceilinged basement filled with rows and rows of filing cabinets. He took her to the area where recent cases were found and led her down an aisle. In a minute he was unlocking a drawer. Elaine stood close beside him when he pulled it out. It was filled with packages wearing red tags that bore a case number and then an exhibit number.

"We'd need a list to know what each number represents."

Elaine reached into the drawer and began squeezing the packages, but she could not find what was certainly a purse. "I can see the purse so plainly as it lay on the table of exhibits at the trial. You'd think I could detect it through a layer of paper."

"We're not even sure it's here. Didn't you come across that list when you made the report?"

She wasn't sure. Women. Phil wondered if she coveted that purse. Well, there was no way she was going to get it. He should have thought of the list before taking her over here. Or she should have. He pushed the drawer shut and locked it.

"Was Jones her real name, Captain?"

"There'd be a court record if she changed it. When and where. We didn't pursue that. No need to."

"How would we have done that?"

"An APB, then hope. My guess would be Vegas."

Finally Elaine tired of talking of the Wilson murder. Murder, not alleged murder. The woman had been tried, convicted, and sentenced and Phil Keegan didn't give a damn about the appeal. Lawyers would enter an appeal for Judas Iscariot. Appeals were a form of legal harassment of the judicial and jury system.

Back in his office he put the Black Museum key in his desk drawer and went off to have a cup of coffee with Cy Horvath.

"Cy, what was Stacey Wilson's name before she changed it?"

"Jones."

"No. I mean before she changed it to Jones?"

Cy's face was impassive through half a minute's thought. "Did she?"

"Just for the fun of it, find out, will you?"

"Vegas?"

"That would be my guess."

Elaine's question had bugged him, as if there was some stone they had left unturned in investigating the murder of Marvin Wilson. Chief Robertson was still sitting on the report, unsure whether to release it to the press. Phil would give him half a day more, then he would leak it. Stacey Wilson's attorneys were already asking what Chief Robertson had to hide.

TWELVE

CY HORVATH felt toward Phil Keegan as a son feels toward his father, which meant that he could see the faults of the man as well as his strengths. Keegan was the best cop Cy knew, but then he was Cy's model, so how could he fail to meet the standard? He was hard-headed, cool-minded, methodical, tenacious. He refused to be deflected by side issues, he kept to the job, he got results.

Usually. Most of the time. It is not in the nature of the job, or of life, to be successful every time. But failure should be explained by factors over which one had no control. Phil Keegan had been a cop a long time and time had taken its toll, no doubt of that. Phil Keegan made mistakes. But Cy Horvath had not imagined he would live long enough to question one of Phil's successes.

The case against Stacey Wilson had been too easy. The pieces fell into place without much effort on their part. Billy Wheaton stuck to his story that Stacey had been in the *Lucky Tyke,* the McNaughtons reluctantly testified that she had been away from the house during the days in question, a massive life insurance policy taken out on Marvin Wilson in her favor came to light. The nature and occasion of the marriage was public knowledge. Phil was right to say the case was open and shut. He was right, too, that Robertson was an idiot to stonewall when the appeal was filed. Finally the chief released the report Elaine had written up but only when he was told it was already in the hands of the press. The beasts in the press room having been fed, Phil was rightly expecting nothing but praise for a job well done, if any stories appeared. The news had been the unavailability of the report. No one but the defense lawyers had professed any interest in its contents.

When Phil asked about Stacey's name before the legal change, Cy didn't want to tell his boss he had already checked out the Vegas courts. He reported to Phil after an hour.

"Already?"

"The fax," Cy said. And that is how he had communicated with Vegas months ago.

"One, the change was made in Vegas. Here's the newspaper item."

He slid the faxed news story he'd just taken from his desk to Keegan. The captain read it with a scowl. It was far from a perfect transmission.

"It doesn't say what her name was."

"That's right."

"Check the court." He tilted the page toward the window and squinted. "Judge Melbourne."

Cy slid two other items toward Keegan. Melbourne's obit and a form from Vegas saying that the records requested could not be provided.

"Why the hell not?"

"Because they don't have them. They're missing. Maybe they don't keep records like that past a certain date. I don't know. Should I pursue it?"

"Does it matter?"

"I don't see how."

"Neither do I."

"What made you wonder about it."

"Elaine asked."

Cy turned to look at the plump young woman plinking away at her computer in the outer office.

"What's this date on these transmissions?" Keegan was holding the fax messages an inch from his nose with his glasses pushed up on his forehead.

"When they were sent."

"February?"

"I wondered at the time."

Cy knew Keegan wouldn't chew him out for it but he didn't like it. He shouldn't. But that was the problem with the Stacey Wilson investigation. They took what was offered them without much questioning. Now Keegan had to wonder why Cy months before and Elaine recently had thought of something he hadn't. So what if it meant nothing? You didn't decide that before the fact. That was what he had learned from Captain Keegan.

They had given Billy Wheaton a bit of a hard time when he placed Mrs. Wilson in the boat, nothing like what the defense lawyers did at the trial, but not just taking the word of a known drunk. Poor Billy had gone on such a toot after the trial he had reeled right out of the world.

Stacey Wilson had insisted she was at the farm all the while her husband was out on his fatal boat ride. The McNaughtons who worked the farm had to testify they could not say she was there.

"You didn't see her?"

"No."

"She didn't ask for any meals to be prepared?"

"No."

"She had no visitors?"

"No."

"Took no phone calls?"

"No."

"Had her bed been slept in?"

"No."

So it had gone at the trial, for both Mr. and Mrs. McNaughton and each question had shot another hole in Stacey's claim to have been at the farm. Why did she say she'd been there when it was so easily disproved? Cy checked the sequence and found that when she made the claim to have been on the farm, Billy Wheaton had not yet come forward. She didn't care whether the story held up, because she didn't think it would matter. If she hadn't been on the boat she could have claimed to be in Las Vegas or on the moon, it wouldn't have mattered as long as she hadn't been placed in the boat with her husband. Cy Horvath could not get rid of the thought that, crazy as her alibi was, it was the lie of a woman innocent of murder, not guilty of it. But if she was not in the boat with Marvin and not in the house, she must have been somewhere and with someone. If not, she'd just say. The only thing that made sense, granting her everything else, was that revealing who that someone was endangered her more than standing trial for murder.

So what would he have done differently if he had been in Keegan's shoes? Talk to Stacey? With her it had been name, rank, and serial number from the start.

Monahan from the prosecutor's office accepted Cy's offer of a drink but when they got across the street to the Pueblo ordered coffee. The bartender looked at him.

"That pot's been brewing since morning."

"Then it ought to be ready."

"What'll you have, Horvath, milk?"

"You got buttermilk?"

"As a matter of fact I do."

"Give me a glass."

The bartender, who could not have remembered it, said it was like Prohibition or something. Nobody drank anymore.

"He should have been with me last night," Monahan said ruefully. "I still can't believe I got through this day. God knows what I did."

"You going to handle our side when the Wilson case comes up?"

"I could handle that one in my sleep. I could have handled it today."

"She's guilty?"

"As charged."

"If she isn't, she sure is dumb."

"Killing her husband is dumb enough."

"No, but think if she really didn't. Just entertain the thought. Geez, we depended on Billy Wheaton. He should have seen two of her if she was in that boat."

Monahan liked that, but laughing made his head ache. The coffee didn't help, but it gave him something to do in a bar that could not bring him further pain.

"Take Billy out of the picture and what do we have? A woman claiming to be where it's easy as pie to show she wasn't."

"Dumb," Monahan agreed.

"She isn't dumb."

Monahan thought about that. "If she's so damned smart why didn't she just enjoy what she had while she had it? He dumps her, it's a golden parachute. She outlives him, she's got it made. Why press matters? Why buy the stupid insurance policy?"

"That's like saying she was at the house."

"Exactly." Monahan paused. "I think."

"Who's she protecting? Or who is a greater threat than life in the slammer?"

"Thank God for Billy Wheaton."

"Yeah. May he rest in peace."

"Amen. Cy, he was the key to our case."

And what would Stacey's story have been if Billy had come forward earlier, before she claimed to have spent those days at the farm? He would have liked to put that question to the lady herself but, one, she wouldn't tell him and, two, he had no excuse to pay her a visit at Joliet.

The booth they sat in gave them a view of the street outside and the courthouse across the street, a convenience for those playing hooky in the Pueblo. As Cy looked across the street, Elaine McCorkle came skipping down the courthouse steps. Cy was struck by the girlishness of her gait and then he saw why. A man awaited her at the foot of the steps. They embraced and then, arms around one another's waists, hips bumping rhythmically, they came across the street. The western sun was on the window through which Cy looked and Elaine couldn't have seen him if she cared, which she obviously didn't. Cy felt a pang of sympathy for the big girl. And then he looked at the man.

The face was familiar. Not because Cy knew the man. But he knew the type.

Looking through a window rendered opaque by sunlight, he might have been looking at the lineup. The similarity tripped a switch and Cy felt a sudden apprehension for Elaine.

"Who are they?" Monahan asked.

"She works for Keegan."

"He's not a cop, is he?"

"No. A robber."

Monahan laughed. The couple passed out of sight.

He spent an hour on the computer, just scanning, concentrating on parole violations, turning up nothing until he expanded the search into neighboring states, juvenile offenders. Before he went home that night, Cy had a make on the man. Tyrone Pajakowski. In trouble with the law since he was a kid. Nothing serious. Not yet. Everything indicated Tyrone's rendezvous with the law would be a lifelong affair. What the hell was Elaine doing with a bum like that? Good-looking, but a bum.

How do you tell a girl who is secretary of the chief of detectives she is going out with a crook? And then it hit Cy. What might be an accident on her part would not be one on his. When he got hold of Keegan he was at St. Hilary's.

"I can't talk, Cy. Roger just had one of his parishioners die."

"Phil, do you know who Elaine's going with?"

"What are you, psychic? The kid who got killed has been taking Elaine out."

"What's his name?"

"Walter, Walter Nickles. I never met him."

"How about Tyrone Pajakowski?"

"Who the hell's he?"

Cy had the odd feeling that he was snitching to the teacher on another kid. But this was something Keegan had to know. An ex-con wouldn't cultivate the secretary of the chief of detectives out of any romantic impulse. He asked Phil if Elaine had done anything odd lately. There was a pause on the line.

"She wanted to see the Black Museum so I took her over and showed it to her."

"She want to see anything in particular?"

"The evidence in the Wilson case." A moment's pause. "Are you at home?"

"I'm still downtown."

"I'll be right there."

"Maybe I better check the Black Museum."

"Wait until I get there."

THIRTEEN

NO MATTER HOW MUCH Elaine tried to tell herself it was just part of her job—after all, Captain Keegan had personally shown her around the Black Museum and had been pretty obvious where the keys were kept—she felt sneaky. Disloyal. She simply would not have done it for anyone other than Tyrone. Aside from liking him as much as she did, how could she fail to be moved by his desire to find in his mother's things something, anything at all, that would verify that he was indeed her son and that she had held him in her arms long, long ago?

Her eyes filled with tears. She felt a bit like a mother to him herself at times. At other times she felt as she had never dared feel toward a man before. And he had changed too. Now that she knew his name was really Tyrone, he seemed to have put away the person he had been as Gordon. Gordon had been shy and seldom spoke, a listener who prompted her to chatter like a teenager about whatever came into her mind. It seemed important to earn the rapt attention with which he listened to everything she said. Tyrone was more forceful, more manly. It was she who kissed Gordon the first time but it was Tyrone who kissed her, sweeping her into his arms so that she felt twenty pounds lighter than she was, felt the weight she ought to be, the weight she would certainly get down to now that she had a real motive for sticking to a diet.

She always started off so well, a glass of gritty liquid for breakfast, another at lunch, and then a sensible dinner. This regimen was supposed to take off a pound a day. And keep it off, as the television spokesmen said—baseball managers, coaches, players themselves. The idea seemed to be that if they could lose weight anyone could. By the third day, Elaine felt so proud of herself she had her sensible meal at lunchtime, at the Great Wall. She tried to find the calorie count of fried rice but it must be right off the chart. The weight she lost in two and a half days was back in one. What was the point? For whom was she becoming slim. Walter? It was easier to think that God meant her to be the weight she was—she felt perfectly comfortable and all her clothes had been bought at this weight. Think of the expense if she really kept to that diet? She could have gained twenty pounds and not worried about losing Walter. But Tyrone provided a motive she just knew would carry her through to victory at last.

And she meant to set his heart at ease about his mother. Her plan was to stay in the office past her usual quitting time, make sure Captain Keegan was gone for the day, then take the keys from his desk.

"There's no need for you to come with me," she had told Tyrone.

"Oh, I have to be there." He took her elbow. "You understand."

But he was a stranger around the department, he would be noticed. People would be so surprised to see her with a man as good-looking as Tyrone they would want to be introduced, Elaine was certain of it. And what if the purse wasn't in the drawer? In that case, she would not want him there. But then she realized that he would find that hard to accept unless he was at her side when she checked the items in his mother's drawer.

"I understand."

It was dumb. She was acting like a woman. She was doing things that made no sense just in order to please a man. How much of that had she seen and read about? Think of the silly girls who were booked every day because of a man's influence over them. Not just uneducated girls, girls with a drug problem—though that had probably been acquired in a dumb effort to impress a man—but women of some sophistication. Elaine had shaken her head in disbelief and here she was doing the same thing.

She had a grudging admiration for Stacey Wilson because she at least had made an effort to be her own person. To use the man rather than vice versa.

Elaine was in the ladies' room, studying herself in the mirror, when this thought occurred. What an awful thought. Imagine using Tyrone... But she could not get rid of the sense that Tyrone was using her.

She went back to her desk where she fussed around, trying to mimic the things she did when she really was leaving for the day. Why were there so many people still here? Honestly, they ought to ring a bell to tell the day people it was time to go home. And then she saw the reason. A death by drowning on South Kinney, with the landlord hysterical.

"Where on South Kinney?" she asked the dispatcher.

"Twenty-one hundreds, in around there."

"Twenty-one hundred what?"

The man looked up at her in surprise. "Don't tell me you live out there."

She knew it before she knew it, Walter's apartment. My God. Drowned in his bathtub. She couldn't believe it.

"Someone you know live there?"

"Walter Nickles."

"That's the guy."

She gave a little dismissive wave of her hand, easy come, easy go, and went back to her desk where she opened the middle drawer and reached way back to the innermost depths and brought out a pack of cigarettes. She had always supplemented her diet by smoking, hating the taste, hating the looks people gave her, never feeling her appetite diminish under the effect of nicotine. Maybe it took a while to work. The smoking stopped with the diet so maybe she had never given it a fair chance.

Now she just wanted something to do. She went back to the ladies' room where she lit a cigarette and squinted at herself in the mirror. She felt nothing. Was it shock? Walter Nickles was dead, drowned in his bathtub, and here she was puffing on a filter cigarette and feeling absolutely nothing at all. Except horror at her own callousness.

Suicide? But wasn't that always some kind of message, a way of getting the last word? Even now, Walter seemed to be trying to get between her and Tyrone. How he had pestered her about Tyrone.

"Elaine, what's he after?"

"What's that supposed to mean?"

"What it says. How many guys like that have you gone with in your life?"

"Meaning he's too good for me?"

"I'll bet you think so. I'll bet you think what a lucky break. Where did he come from? What does he want?"

"Are you through flattering me?"

Walter knew her all too well. Of course she found it hard to believe that Tyrone could actually be drawn to her. What girl wouldn't respond to his attentions? Tyrone was certainly after something, he had been all along. Elaine lit another cigarette, faced herself in the mirror. Truth time.

He looked me up because he knew I worked for Captain Keegan. The supermarket line? He arranged that. He saw where I shopped, got into line just before I did, the rest, apparently all so happenstance, followed. *He is using me.* She formed the words but did not speak them aloud. Smoke slid from her mouth, a coded version of the thought. What he wanted all along was to get at his mother's things that were still in police custody. Walter, sliding beneath the water of his bathtub, was getting the last word after all.

The image startled her and for the first time she faced the reality of Walter's death. The mellifluous voice would persuade no one else to subscribe to magazines they had no real need or desire for.

The little flurry over the suicide of Walter Nickles had subsided and the day crew was gone when Elaine went into Captain Keegan's office, opened his desk, and took the keys from where she had seen him put them. She took the elevator to the basement. Tyrone was waiting for her there, an eager expression on his face.

"Do you have the keys?"

She nodded. "Word just came in upstairs. Walter Nickles is dead."

"Walter Nickles."

"The man who threatened you."

Then he remembered. "Dead?"

"Drowned."

"It's pretty early for swimming, isn't it?"

"In his bathtub."

"Come on."

"Apparently it was suicide."

"Because of us?"

Us. What did that mean? This was not the time or place to pursue it.

"Come."

She set off through the tunnel to the building across the street, Tyrone beside her. The farther into it they got, the greater the echo their footsteps created. Elaine felt now that she was involved in a fated action, beyond choice. Was this what he had been aiming at all along? His polite detachment when she talked to him of her job was transparent now. Would he, if they found the purse, go away and never be seen again?

When she let them into the vast warehouse filled with its rows and rows of cabinets, his breath escaped him in a low whistle.

"Do you know where it is?"

She might have pretended to search for it, to prolong the moment, but now she wanted only to get this over with. She felt that Walter was there with them, an observer from wherever he was now. There would a funeral! How could she possibly go?

Tyrone marched beside her with military precision to the aisle in which the Wilson materials were filed. She went to the appropriate drawer as if she had been there many times before. The first attempt to put the key in failed. She turned it over, slipped it in, and unlocked the drawer. Tyrone waited patiently for her to open it.

"There they are."

She had expected him to plunge his hands in and start tearing open packages but he waited for her. It was different from the time she had been here with Captain Keegan. The package with the purse in it seemed to seek out her hand.

"I'm sure this is it."

"Will you open it?"

The package. Isn't that why they had come? But she lifted the Scotch tape carefully from the paper and opened it. The purse was a bit of a disappointment in this light. Its clasps seemed tarnished. She handed it to Tyrone.

"You open it."

There was a satisfying click as the two parts of the clasp disengaged. The purse did not open wide. Tyrone's hand slid into it and came out again almost immediately, holding what looked like a calling card. He drew it out with his index and middle fingers, like a pickpocket.

"What's that?"

He showed her, then put his hand back in the purse. "I'm looking for photographs."

Charge cards, credit cards, lipstick, a makeup brush, tissues, the usual odds and ends of a woman's purse. "No photographs."

"It's not the kind of purse that holds much." She looked into his disappointed face. What had he hoped to find? Surely no photograph could have provided the sense he wanted that he belonged to someone, that he had a mother.

"Go see her, Tyrone. Visit her."

His chin touched his chest. Then he nodded. "I'll think about it."

"Do you want to look at anything else?"

He shook his head. "Thanks, Elaine."

She rewrapped the purse and put it back into the drawer. "I wish there'd been better results."

He squeezed her arm and it seemed more expressive of affection than a kiss. When she locked the drawer and they moved out of the aisle she felt a sudden relief. She had done what Tyrone had asked, it was all over, and what real harm had there been?

They went silently into the tunnel but after a few steps, Tyrone stopped. "Did you hear something?" He spoke in a whisper.

There was a sound behind them and Elaine turned to see Captain Keegan standing just inside the warehouse.

"Elaine?"

"Captain Keegan. Good Lord, you frightened us."

There were sounds in the tunnel as well and Cy Horvath came into sight. His approach had the effect of shepherding Elaine and Tyrone toward Captain Keegan and soon the four of them were standing in the warehouse.

"This is a friend of mine," Elaine began.

"Tyrone Pajakowski," Cy Horvath said.

"That's right. How did you know? Tyrone, this is Captain Keegan, I've told you about him, and this is Lieutenant Horvath."

"What are you doing here at this time of day?" Keegan asked.

"Oh, for heaven's sake. I was showing Tyrone the Black Museum is all."

"Anything in particular?"

"The Wilson stuff. Captain Keegan, it's okay. Stacey Wilson is Tyrone's mother."

FOURTEEN

WALTER NICKLES was found in his condo in Mallard Estates, five lean buildings standing on a scalped landscape looking forlornly at an artificial lake on which, such had been the developer's idea, the eponymous mallard would float. Rain had made runnels in the land sloping toward the lake but the water level was very low, suggesting to Father Dowling a basin of water with a loose plug. Would the setting of Walter's life have seemed so bleak if he had not come on so grim a mission?

The body was still in the tub, Derek Hart, the medical examiner, having declared him dead as soon as he checked the vital signs, kneeling beside the tub in the bathroom that must have been designed by a computer programmed for undersize adults.

"How long?" Roger Dowling asked.

Hart shrugged, as if sensing a metaphysical question in the offing. "Hours?"

Roger Dowling gave him a blessing anyway, the one Walter had thought he was receiving the first time they met. He was wearing shorts, a decorous note, and was folded into the tub, lying on his back, his shoulders flat against the bottom of the tub, his knees angled high above the rim. It would have been impossible for a man Walter's size simply to slide under the water in so small a tub. Perhaps the effort it cost to get his head under water had distracted him from what he was doing.

Father Dowling joined Officer Agnes Lamb who was standing by until Hart and his assistant finished their work.

"Was he a parishioner, Father?"

"I'd met him. He wanted to be a monk."

Agnes looked inscrutably at him.

"He was in love with Phil Keegan's secretary."

"Elaine McCorkle?"

"She had found another man. He wanted to enter the monastery and join the Church, in which order he wasn't quite sure."

Agnes looked over Hart's head at the body, which had been removed from the tub and lay upon the floor as more photographs were taken. Walter's legs and feet extended out of the room.

Given the seriousness of things they had spoken of, Roger Dowling was surprised at how little he knew of the man. It was clear that Walter had worked out of his apartment. A second bedroom was an office: a trestle desk, computer, and elaborate telephone with a headset that would have left Walter's hands free to make entries in the computer as he talked. Father Dowling noticed that there were no magazines in the apartment and very few books. These were paperbacks, chunky glittering stories of international intrigue, spies, betrayals. Their covers promised stories of a world seconds away from nuclear destruction and declared that they had been runaway bestsellers. Runaway bestsellers had kept Walter at home even when he wasn't on the phone. In the bedroom a framed certificate announced that Walter Nickles was qualified in SALES AND LEADERSHIP. Father Dowling tipped back his head to read the whole legend. It seemed to commemorate a two-day seminar at the O'Hare Inn conducted by Brad Crispin & Associates. Had Walter hidden it in the bedroom because he knew what it was worth? Or did he want his waking eye to rest upon its reassuring message?

Evidence of a family in Helena, Montana, was turned up in the kitchen. Agnes was examining two or three letters, busy with her task; Roger felt superfluous now. He looked around the apartment before leaving. Why did the place depress him so? He was certain it would have even if he was not seeing it in such grim circumstances. Imagine the fellow priests who would regard his rectory and parish as the archdiocesan pits, yet it was at St. Hilary's that, for the first time, he had found what he had wanted all along, doing the essential work of the priest, saying Mass, dispensing the sacraments, baptizing, marrying, burying. His routine kept vividly before him the entry and exit points of life and how insignificant sometimes seemed the years in between. No, he rejected the thought. If one had to be a world historical figure in order to lead a significant life, the vast majority of humans were condemned to pointless durations. But what are the criteria of historical importance? Monsters and heroes have an equal claim on the historian's attention because their lives affect the lives of millions of others, and seldom for the good. It was the *how* far more than the *what* that mattered. But there was nothing to prevent Walter from having become a moral hero by doing well the things he had done. There was nothing to prevent him from becoming a saint.

An abject Marie Murkin awaited him at the rectory, her face a tragic mask.

"It's my fault, Father."

"What have you done?"

"Walter Nickles. If only I had kept my nose out of their affairs."

"Marie, you had absolutely nothing to do with his death."

"It was suicide?"

"Apparently."

She lifted her hands as if he had confirmed her claim to responsibility.

"Next you'll be saying Elaine is responsible."

Marie was obviously struck for the first time by Elaine's prior and stronger claim to have driven Walter Nickles to suicide. Indeed, her own case depended on Elaine's guilt. This brought Marie back to her senses.

"Nonsense." She smoothed her apron. "We all have free will, Father Dowling."

"So I was always taught. I only doubt it when you ask me to quit drinking coffee and stop smoking."

"Kill yourself if you want to," Marie said cheerfully.

"I read the other day that bread is full of cancer-causing agents."

"I don't believe it."

"That I read it or that it's true?"

But she was not to be distracted. "Bread is the staff of life."

"That's catchy."

Her face grew suddenly long again. "Will his funeral be here?"

"He wasn't Catholic."

An antinomian mood took momentary possession of her. "Does it really matter? Give him the works."

"His family might not like that."

She reacted equivocally to the news of the relatives in Helena, as if they were trying to horn in on her plans to waive Church law and respect for the deceased and lay on a funeral Mass for the repose of his soul.

"He came to you, Father. Isn't that a sign of baptism of desire."

He resisted saying that Walter's baptismal font might have been the tub in which he drowned. Roger Dowling was skeptical of near-death stories, people who all but died and spoke of the experience with great vividness. But surely there could be a moment before the light of this world died and that of the other dawned when the suicide could repent. It was good to see Marie so eager to get Walter into the church *in ictu mortis,* as the moral theologians used to say. She was always grumbling about people like Frank Sinatra who after rich and unedifying lives and lots of wives were reconciled to the faith of their fathers. In their case, Marie wanted public penance, a confession of faults, sackcloth, and ashes.

AT NINE THAT EVENING Phil arrived at the rectory and joined the pastor in the study. The Cubs had been rained out and Roger had not expected to see his old friend. It was then that he heard the strange story of Tyrone Pajakowski, Elaine, and the Black Museum.

"Women," Phil said with disgust.

"God bless them," Marie said, appearing in the doorway. "I thought I heard your voice." She wore a housecoat and large bunny slippers and looked like a gray-haired little girl.

"Phil has no beer."

"I'd rather have some whiskey."

Once Roger Dowling had known that desire, but in his case it had been a desire for oblivion, flight from the agony of the marriage tribunal and all its insoluble problems. It was otherwise with Phil, who could have a drink and stop. For whatever reason, that had been a knack Roger Dowling lost and he had quit drinking entirely. And like most former drinkers he made up for it with coffee and tobacco.

"Is he really Stacey Wilson's son?"

"It's possible. Cy tracked down a bailiff in Las Vegas who remembered what she changed her name from when she became Stacey Jones. The records weren't kept and the judge is dead. Anyone but Cy might have let it go."

"But it could be a coincidence that both are Pajakowskis?"

"That would be more likely if it were publicly known that was her name. The fact that he knew it is significant."

"What was it he wanted?"

"Some proof she was his mother. Or so he told Elaine."

"Was there any?"

"They both say no."

"Has he visited her?"

"Yup."

"So you can ask her?"

"Cy will. He's done everything else, let him tie it up. The son, if that's what he is, has spent most of his life on the wrong side of the law. Juvenile offenses, reform school, time for a stolen vehicle but that was a plea bargain."

"You think that he deliberately cultivated Elaine?"

"You've met Elaine. Men aren't breaking down her door, Roger."

"Just Walter Nickles."

"Isn't life a screwed-up mess?

"It's what we make it."

"That's what I said."

FIFTEEN

TUTTLE STOOD by the downtown Picasso and looked across the street at the building that housed the offices of Stacey Wilson's defense lawyers. It had never been Tuttle's aspiration to have digs like those: it would mean partners, associates, paralegals, secretaries. A secretary he could use. His last had left threatening to sue him for back wages. But which of his confreres would take such a case? If he couldn't pay his secretary, what could they squeeze out of him? Besides, he himself had typed out an elaborate IOU. No one could say he shirked his debts. Tuttle glanced once more at the Picasso and shook his head. Some of the people all of the time. He adjusted his tweed hat, patted the pocket containing the cassettes, and crossed the street, darting among the honking cars.

Burke, Rusk, Wong & Wagner were on the twenty-third floor. Tuttle felt like an astronaut when he came into the extensive reception area.

"Wong?" he asked the receptionist after reeling off the names.

"No, you're right. This is the place."

"I meant Wong." He pointed to the names mounted on the wall behind her.

"Is he expecting you?"

"I'm here to see Jewel."

She frowned. Tuttle decided he could do without a receptionist too after his ship came in. He was reminded of the bitch in Amos Cadbury's office in Fox River.

The receptionist invited Tuttle to take a seat. He took a seat. Fifteen minutes passed. Then a young girl came up to him.

"Mr. Tuttle?"

"That's me."

"I'll take your hat."

"I'll keep it." But he took it off. "It contains all my bugging equipment."

Her lids permanently concealed the upper third of her eyes, giving her a contemplative look.

"What do you do here?"

"I'm Melanie Jewel."

A dame! What was this? He expected to talk with Hasser or Lowell who had appeared in court, not some kid. He came to a halt. "I'm supposed to deal with you?"

"If you deal at all."

He shook his head and put his hat back on. "Uh-uh. Hasser or Lowell or no deal."

"What is the deal you keep talking about?"

He hesitated. A winning hand is strongest when nothing is showing. "Tapes."

"Then you do bug?"

"You're doing all right yourself."

She laughed. Feet apart, hands holding the lapels of her chalkstripe suit. She looked about seventeen years old.

"Come on. We'll call Mr. Hasser from my office."

"Are you a lawyer?"

"Yes."

Dear God. She looked like a high school kid—except for the suit. "So am I."

"I know."

"Word of mouth is the best advertising."

No comment. Working in this firm where business probably flowed through the doors, she would have no conception of what a rat race it was out there for your average attorney. And for Tuttle too, who did not consider himself average. A life builds toward a big moment that will define everything up to that point as well as afterward. He might have been addressing his late father.

"Tuttle and Tuttle," he told Jewel. "Fox River."

Behind her desk, she jotted something on a pad. His name? "Please." She indicated a chair. "Now what precisely should I tell Mr. Hasser when I call him."

"That Mr. Tuttle is here."

She nodded and took a note. "About some cassettes."

"That should prove useful in the Stacey Wilson appeal."

That was the Open Sesame. She picked up the phone and conveyed this message to Hasser through his secretary and in a minute Hasser appeared, taking a chair next to Tuttle's after a perfunctory handshake. The two men looked at Jewel as if they were consulting her.

"Mr. Tuttle practices law in Fox River. He has some cassettes that he feels may be helpful in the Stacey Wilson appeal."

"Cassettes of what?" He put the question to Jewel.

"You can talk to me direct," Tuttle said. "No charge."

Jewel stifled a laugh. Hasser looked at Tuttle closely. "I never met you all the weeks I argued that case. I never heard your name mentioned."

"In a murder trial? I hope not."

Hasser glanced at Jewel who was making more noise not laughing than if she'd let herself go.

"What I have is a tape I made of an interview with Billy Wheaton. Him being dead now, you may want testimony in his own voice."

"When did you interview Wheaton?"

Tuttle took out the cassettes and wasted a lot of time looking them over. He read the date off the cassette marked *Billy*.

"What are the others?"

"The McNaughtons."

"So you got the three witnesses that lost my case for me."

"How interested in these tapes would you be if it weakens or reverses their testimony?"

"What did you do, threaten them?"

"With what?"

Hasser thought about it. "I won't ask if you paid them." He glanced at Jewel but got no laugh. He tipped back in his chair, considered the ceiling, looked steadily at Tuttle, and then spoke in the direction of the window behind Jewel. Older lawyer showing younger lawyer how it is done. Big-city lawyer condescending to suburban town lawyer.

"Quite aside from the fact that it is unlikely to the point of impossibility to get tapes admitted as evidence—"

"I didn't say I'd make it easy for you. Maybe I can make it possible."

Hasser didn't appreciate the interruption. "Tapes can be faked, edited."

"There was a witness."

"Your wife."

"I don't have a wife." Tuttle smiled at Jewel. "It was a cop."

"A cop."

"An officer of the Fox River police."

"Interesting."

Tuttle shoved the cassettes back into his pocket and stood. "Apparently not to you. Okay, I'll check it out with Mrs. Wilson. I think the defendant ought to decide on matters of importance, don't you?"

"Sit down."

"I'm wasting your time, you're wasting mine."

Hasser stood and said to Jewel, "Get something to play those on and bring it to my office. Mr. Tuttle and

I will be there." He bowed to Tuttle and made a sweeping gesture toward the door. "*Après vous, monsieur.*"

"*Muchas gracias.*"

SIXTEEN

AT JOLIET Tyrone was admitted to the visiting room to see Shirley Langer, who had worked in the kitchen in Stillwater where she apparently learned the attractions of crime. She'd been caught on her first try, an attempt on a pizza delivery vehicle, and had only months before parole.

"You ever seen Stacey Wilson?" Tyrone asked.

"That your idea of a hello?" Part of being in prison was pretending you were horny all the time.

"I don't like to rush things."

"You still waiting for me?"

"How many others are?"

She got serious. "Write me, Tyrone. Send me your picture. Promise?"

He put his hand against the wire and she flattened hers against it, closing her eyes and groaning.

"On one condition."

"Name it."

"Get Stacey out here."

"How'n the hell'm I gonna do that?"

"Tell her her kid brother's here."

"Tyrone. I go back I can't come out again today. You know that."

"Tomorrow send her out."

"Ask for her."

"I'll ask for you, but it's her I expect to see."

She was free from him in prison, that's how he felt. He had to return to the uncertainties of the outside world armed only with the card he'd palmed from her purse. Anastasie Caisse-Epargne. It sounded like some broad, but of course it had to be a bank, a Swiss bank. A series of paired digits that suggested a telephone number must be the account number. So he had the key to the money she had squirreled away, but how was he supposed to turn it? As a precaution against losing that number, he carefully copied it out twice where he would be able to find it. Once on page 71 of *Huckleberry Finn,* a book he read at least once a year. He also wrote the string of numbers at the beginning of the Book of Revelation in the Bible he'd lifted from a motel. He had a feeling Horvath was going to find out about that missing card so he returned it to Elaine.

"I thought you put it back."

"Will you?"

The thought of returning to that room full of cabinets recalled to her the encounter with Horvath and Keegan.

"Tyrone, I'm so sorry."

"It's my fault. What the hell difference does it make who my mother is?"

"Don't say that." She looked at the card and then excitedly at him. "Maybe this is her."

"That's French."

She searched his features as if for signs of French origin. He stuck out his tongue. A waste. She didn't get it.

"You look as French as you do Polish."

"What nationality are you?"

"German mostly. It goes back so far it doesn't matter."

"Keegan give you a hard time today?"

"Worse. He never mentioned it."

"It's really no big deal, Elaine. So you wanted to show off working for the cops for a guy you're going with."

"Am I going with you?"

"If you hurry."

He was reassured by her manner. The night before she had been like a kid caught stealing candy. Keegan did the talking, but it was Horvath Tyrone was conscious of. He was sure he'd seen that big monkey before. Keegan was very calm, very concise. The Black Museum was off limits except to badged policemen. He pocketed without comment the keys Elaine gave him.

"You here to look up something, Captain?" Tyrone asked. He was playing the dumb innocent but he wanted to know what had brought these two at this particular moment.

It was Horvath who answered. "I'll go get it, Captain. Give me the keys."

Smooth but not smooth enough. They'd been watching Elaine. That meant they had been watching the two of them together. And that most likely meant that they had identified Tyrone Pajakowski.

"How long have you been in town?" Keegan asked before he let them go.

"That depends."

And he looked sheepishly at Elaine. Who giggled. Like a schoolgirl. My God. Then hand in hand the two of them went back down the tunnel, through the courthouse, and into the street. Once outside, Elaine began to tremble with delayed nerves.

"What a time for those two to show up."

"History is a series of accidents."

Aphorisms were wasted on her. He took her home and on the doorstep shook her hand, meaning it as a kind of joke, but she pumped his up and down, obviously anxious to get away.

And two days later, after a movie, he suggested they go to his place. Her mouth opened but closed before she said anything. She gave a little shake of her head.

"I couldn't."

"Let me be the judge of that."

"No. The funeral is tomorrow. I have to go."

Walter Nickles. Tyrone told her he had forgotten all about him. "What a waste," he said.

She squeezed his hand as if he had expressed regret for Walter Nickles's sake.

"SHE SENT A QUESTION and then a message," Shirley Langer told him when he went back to Joliet.

"I want to see her."

"She won't come. You know why. Her words."

"What's the question?"

"Did you get the card?"

"What's the message?"

"Number it among your most precious possessions."

"Shirley, tell her I don't know how to use it."

She looked dumbly at him, but he was the one who was dumb. Shirley was just a messenger—like a telephone wire, she didn't know the meaning of what she told him.

"Okay, I'll tell her."

"And tell her I'll number it among my most precious memories."

"Possessions."

"Devils."

She made a face.

"Word associations. Haven't they played that game with you yet? Stillwater."

"Runs deep." Her face broke into a smile. She had surprised herself.

He put his hand to the screen and she pressed hers against it.

"Palm."

"Tree."

"Adam."

"Apple."

"Gulp."

"Gulp? That's not a word."

"To anyone. Good-bye."

SEVENTEEN

WALTER NICKLES'S cousin from Montana was named Hagerty, his wife was Charlotte, and they assured Marie they would be delighted if Father Dowling would have a little service at McDivitt's before the body was taken to the cemetery.

"You're not taking the body back to Montana?"

"That boy hasn't seen Montana since he was eight years old."

"My sister and her man just had to move East," Charlotte said, shaking her head. Marie had never heard Illinois referred to as the East before.

"Did they live in Fox River?"

"We never heard of Fox River until the police contacted us. They always told us they lived in Chicago."

"This is Chicago," Marie said, meaning the archdiocese.

"Fox River a suburb?"

Marie nodded vaguely. There were no witnesses to the conversation and the niceties of geography seemed a small thing. Marie liked the Hagertys.

"With a name like that you two must be Catholic."

They both looked alarmed and shook their heads.

"Your father then?" she said to him.

"My father was more likely to be in a whorehouse than a church."

"Mitch," Charlotte cried, punching him in the arm. She made a face at Marie. "That's Montana for you."

Despite this extraordinary remark, Marie went on liking them. She didn't care what Mitchell Hagerty said, there had to be Catholics in his background. That was no Orangeman's name, if she knew anything about it.

Father Dowling refused to be elated when she gave him the good news.

"Did you talk them into it?"

"Their name is Hagerty!"

"Catholics?"

"They say not."

"Do you think they're lying?"

"I suppose everybody goes back to Catholics, don't they? Before Luther and that."

"I had no idea you were such a historian."

"Everybody knows that."

Of course he did what the Hagertys wanted, and did a very nice job too. Marie was a student of the various undertakers, whose calling brought them into contact with the parish, and her present inclination was to leave instructions that McDivitt be entrusted with her own funeral arrangements. By this time she knew better than to say anything to Roger Dowling. The man could be such a tease, especially when he thought she was overdramatizing. But surely a person had an obligation to look ahead, make arrangements, be less of a burden to others after she was gone. And wasn't it human to imagine what others might think and say when there was no more Marie Murkin?

It was her cross that no one seemed as aware as she was how much the smooth running of the parish depended on her. In a secondary way, of course; she wasn't what Father Dowling called usurping. McDivitt expected last-minute instructions from her now, and people in the parish, the old timers at least, had sense enough to go through her if they wanted fast action from the pastor. If the service at the funeral home took place it was because she'd had the good sense to broach the matter with the Hagertys. She wasn't looking for credit or praise, but wasn't it much better this way?

Elaine McCorkle was there, trying to be invisible. My, what a large girl she had become. Take off some of that weight and with her face she'd be a pretty thing. She'd been pretty enough the way she was for Walter Nickles, poor fellow. Grief rose suddenly in Marie at the thought of that poor cast-off fellow doing away with himself in the bathtub because Elaine did not love him.

Father Dowling had blamed her, she had blamed herself, for speaking to Elaine about her praying to St. Anthony, but wouldn't everything be better now if the girl had stayed with Walter?

"I wonder who the other man is?" Marie had asked Father Dowling.

"A crook, in Phil Keegan's words."

"Are you serious?"

"It's doubtful that he is about her. Phil thinks he's been cultivating Elaine for a purpose. He's probably already left town."

Of course Elaine hadn't brought him to the funeral service. How pitiable if she had been deceived by the other man and now had no one. The girl ought to have a good cry, get it out of her system, not just sit there with that dumb expression on her doughy face.

Marie had explained to the Hagertys that she couldn't be coming on to the cemetery, she had to get back to the rectory. But they could count on Father Dowling. When Father Dowling had closed his book and asked everyone—everyone!—to join him in saying the Lord's Prayer, Elaine slipped out, but Marie was right on her heels.

"Elaine," she called in a funeral parlor whisper. The girl turned with a guilty expression on her wide face.

"Marie Murkin," She took the girl's hand.

"Yes. I remember."

"I meant to do good."

"I understand."

"I'm so glad you came, particularly now."

"What do you mean?"

My, what a sensitive thing she was. "Well, you weren't going with him anymore."

"No."

"Did you hear he wanted to become a monk?"

"What?"

"He must have thought it was the Foreign Legion. He came to the rectory and said he wanted to enter a monastery."

They had reached the parking lot now and Elaine began to shake. She was laughing and crying too, tears rolling down her cheeks.

"He was such a nerd." She spoke with affection.

Marie decided not to risk telling Elaine she mustn't blame herself.

"Just you don't run off to the convent now."

"That'll be the day."

"Thank God you've found Mr. Right."

"You seem to know all about me." The girl's tone was not especially complimentary.

"It's working at the rectory, Elaine. You can imagine. And Captain Keegan is an old friend of Father's."

Elaine got into her car without a further word and pulled the door shut with a bang. Marie had been about to ask her for a lift to the rectory. She sighed and got out of the way so Elaine could back up. Marie was left standing in the middle of the parking lot.

She looked heavenward, offering it up, and started off on the four-block walk—long blocks—to St. Hilary's.

EIGHTEEN

THE ST. HILARY SCHOOL was no longer a school because of the demographic changes that had taken place in the parish. Most of the young had fled to the suburbs when the parish was literally triangulated by the interstate and two expressways. Now young families were buying and redecorating the fine old homes and when their children were a little older the school might come into existence again, but for the nonce, as the pastor put it, it would be a center for senior parishioners. Edith Hospers had run the center from its inception, and it was her secret prayer that it would never become a school again.

"Where would we get the nuns?" she asked Father Dowling.

"Good question."

"Even starvation wages for lay teachers would run to a fortune."

"Wages like yours?"

"Father, you know how content I am with this job. Please don't think I'm angling for anything. I'd do it for less."

"Not if I have anything to say about it."

He had dreamed up the center when he spoke to her about what she would do after Earl had done those dreadful things and was sent to prison. Edith wondered how many knew the whereabouts of her husband. She didn't mind Father Dowling knowing—where would she be if he hadn't known?—but it bothered her that others should know and talk about it. Not because of herself, but because of the children. Earl had never let her take any of them to see him.

"Tell them I'm dead."

"I will not!"

"I'll be as good as dead by the time I get out of here."

Edith still felt a terrible loneliness without him but she had grown used to his absence too, grown used to loneliness, she supposed, and talking of when he would get out was like talking of Santa Claus to the kids. The kids seemed to take knowing that their father was in prison without visible strain. She knew nothing of psychology but there were times she wondered what thoughts festered in the silence of their minds, below conscious level, breeding God knew what effects in the future.

"Everyone has skeletons in their closet, Edith," Father Dowling said. "Adam and Eve, at least."

That was when he told her there were things in his own past he was ashamed of. She couldn't imagine him drinking too much, but he wouldn't have made up something like that. She had never known anyone so serene, so levelheaded.

"You always know what to say, Father."

"Edith, I'm not a counselor. I'm a priest. The talk's a bonus. If I were deaf and dumb it wouldn't matter."

If there was anything about working at St. Hilary's that never got easier it was Marie Murkin. The woman had to be a pain in the neck to Father Dowling too, but he never gave any indication of it. Marie was so nosy. She never exactly said that Edith owed her regular reports on how things were going at the center, but whenever she showed up in Edith's office, all sweetness and goo, it was clear she wanted to be brought up to date.

"Elaine came to the services at McDivitt's and I suppose that was a good thing."

"Many people there?"

"You were missed, Edith." Marie had suggested on the phone that it might be a good thing to have a St. Hilary's contingent, but backed off when Edith asked if this was the pastor's idea.

"I would have been missed here too."

"Any calls while I was gone?"

Marie had rerouted the rectory phone to the center while she was at McDivitt's. "Nothing for you."

"I didn't mean personal calls."

"When does Father Dowling hear confessions?"

"Edith, just ask."

"Not for myself. Someone called to ask that."

Marie sighed. "I've tried to convince Father Dowling to make a little recording of when Mass is said, when confessions heard, what arrangements for marriage and funerals, but he won't hear of it. If the caller didn't hang up after that, we'd answer. Most parishes have such a message."

"I'd hate to have to listen to that every time I called the rectory."

"That's the hitch. Phil Keegan says the same thing."

Captain Keegan had represented the enemy during Earl's troubles and Edith had never gotten over the hatred she had felt for him then. But him she could avoid. Marie was part of the job.

"I thought Elaine had a new boyfriend."

"Father Dowling says he's a crook. Quoting Captain Keegan. Some boyish misdeeds, no doubt."

Marie was back that afternoon, to give rather than to get news.

"Edith, you won't believe this. The new boyfriend of Elaine's? He claims to be the son of Stacey Wilson."

"Claims? Why would he say a thing like that?"

Marie threw up her hands. "God knows."

She was off to the rectory then, and Edith went down the corridor to the former gym where fierce games of bridge and 500 were in progress. She really didn't have time to think of what Marie had said but it worked on her mind the rest of the day. It was crazy to think that Marie had acted as if this was news Edith would particularly want to know. Earl's imprisonment. Stacey Wilson's, and now the man Captain Keegan's secretary had dumped Walter Nickles for—

all of them in trouble with the law—it all added up to what Edith would want to know.

She saw the minibus turn in and went outside where Karen was already helping her charges out of the vehicle, bought for a song from a rental car company that had used it to ferry customers from the airport terminal to their lot. The vehicle hadn't been made for long trips.

"How was it?" Edith asked. Bernadette Kilmartin humphed as she shuffled by, but she hadn't approved of anything yet, and had probably gone on the trip to the Shedd Aquarium only to put her stamp of disapproval on such outings.

The five others in the group gave it their okay. Old Mr. McGrade had loaded up on free literature which he held up like a winning hand.

"They loved it," Karen said. "It's a long ride, but they liked the aquarium itself."

"The minibus handle all right?"

"It runs like a watch. But people think I made a wrong turn somewhere." They had painted out the name of the car rental company but its distinctive colors remained.

Edith got in and rode around behind the school with Karen.

"We should have had that luggage rack removed when the seat belts were installed."

"I'd vote for shorter trips. Know what Bernadette said?"

"Tell me."

"She'd rather go look at the Wilson farm."

The suggestion had been made that they visit the local courts when trials were on, but Edith thought that was the sort of thing old people did on their own.

"Try to think of some closer attractions."

"Great America."

"I'd like to see Bernadette on the roller coaster."

Karen had thick reddish hair, and was almost as tall as Edith. She was a volunteer who had come to work in January when she graduated from Loyola.

"I told Father Dowling I'd give it a year."

Edith doubted that Karen would stay that long. The old people loved her enthusiasm and energy, and Edith was delighted to have full-time help in diverting the senior parishioners. Most important, Karen did not condescend or make the old people feel they were children. It turned out that her volunteer year was meant to make up for a grandfather Karen felt she had neglected, too busy going to school to spend time with him during his last days.

"Of course I never said it or explicitly thought it, but I know I wished he'd hurry up about it and not be such a drain on my parents, particularly my mother."

"Did he live with you?"

"Are you kidding? Mom and Dad both work and my sister and I were in college. I don't understand it, but he turned over whatever he had and became a ward of the state. I don't think I visited him a dozen times."

"But you did visit him?"

"Grudgingly. Until the end. One day he told me it wouldn't be long, as if he were apologizing. It knocked me over. A human person saying he's sorry to be alive and cluttering up the earth! He didn't invent old age."

She went on and Edith didn't understand all of it—Karen was still suffering from her education, as the pastor put it—but she knew then that Karen would be with her a year. That she could afford to work a year without pay surprised Edith.

"I won't tell you what I could have been earning this year. Well, I'll start earning next year."

This had suggested that like short-term volunteers Karen had a voyeur's interest in the elderly, but the story of her grandfather corrected that impression.

"It's not a very exciting life, Karen."

"Oh, I don't know. Some of these old guys look pretty cute."

"After a while they don't even look old."

Now in April, Edith felt she knew Karen pretty well, but she didn't know if there was a man in her life. Edith's case was different. Made a widow of sorts by Earl's conviction, that side of her life had simply ceased. She had married Earl for better or worse and got the worse, so how could she complain? Father Dowling was a celibate, Marie Murkin was whatever she was, the senior parishioners were flirty and carried on funny little romances among themselves, but they were over the hill in that department too. But Karen, a beautiful bright young woman, should have a man. Edith's hints to this effect got through.

"Jane Austen."

Edith looked at her. Odd remarks usually got explained if she waited.

"'It is a truth universally recognized that a single man...' And the same for girls."

"What's wrong with that?"

"Edith, I'm not a nun."

Karen's laugh and Karen's smile lit up the place, and they were almost an excuse for having pried into her life.

NINETEEN

AMOS CADBURY was the senior surviving member of the three lawyers who had founded Fox River's most prestigious law firm and he was still active. He continued to look after the legal affairs of those who had been his clients for years, and he was trustee of many estates. He had become venerable with age and, though he would never have claimed it even in the privacy of his own conscience, he had become wise. He thought of his wisdom as merely commonplace truths gleaned from long experience.

Aristotle had said that most men are bad, and he had no conception of Original Sin. Amos, who did, thought that most men were foolish, using 'men' as it had always been used, to mean all human beings. And the folly of mankind is nowhere more evident than in matters of money. To those who saw sex as occupying pride of place, Amos was ready to grant much, but not its primacy. In his experience more harm came about through money—its pursuit, its custody, its passing on, and all the rest of it. The appearance of William Sibley in his office did not shake his conviction on the matter.

Sibley wore what it pained Amos to think were fashionable clothes, a loose-fitting double-breasted jacket that seemed designed for a watermelon thief, an open shirt of orangish color, which exposed a thick gold necklace. His face was made narrower by the way his hair was worn, swept back from the face and apparently highly greased. Amos reminded himself that Sibley had flown in from California and was seated in his office only because of the recommendation of an associate in Los Angeles.

"You are the son of Lydia Wilson nee Gardner?" She was Marvin's first wife, who had killed herself some years after their divorce.

"Stepson."

"Then you are Marvin Wilson's son."

"I am the child she had by the man she married before she married Marvin Wilson."

"I see."

It was Amos's profession to help clients arrange for the posthumous disposition of their wealth. Given a donor, a recipient is implied. There is no moral fault associated with being the heir of other's money—Amos had a preference for old money, if only because its holders were used to it, jaded in their affluence—but there is something unsavory in an eager claimant. And in William Sibley's case, it was difficult to see what his claim was.

"If Marvin Wilson left no will, my mother would have a claim, wouldn't she?"

"They were divorced."

"But if there were no other heirs."

"And you of course represent yourself as your mother's heir."

"Exactly."

"So at three removes, you wish to regard yourself as Marvin Wilson's heir?"

"What do you think?"

Amos Cadbury did not like his advice asked as if he were recommending a horse in the third race at Arlington.

"What do you do, Mr. Sibley?"

"I'm a media consultant."

"That sounds as though you read tea leaves."

"I put TV packages together—actors, writers, producers, financial types."

"Are you successful?"

"It's a crowded field, but I do all right."

"Your survival does not depend on the success of your claim?"

"You don't think I have a chance."

"On the contrary. The Wilson estate is so jumbled now that anything might happen. Judges do not as a rule like to see money go undistributed. Nor does the IRS. They have to know whom to tax. Your claim is antic enough to fit right in."

"Will you represent me?"

"Yes." Amos stood and extended his hand across the desk. Sibley took it and applied a strong grip. Amos sat down. "I will need your mother's marriage certificates. Both of them. All of them. I will need your birth certificate. I suppose I should have your father's marriage certificate as well."

"You mean my Sibley father or my real father?"

"Isn't the man by whom Lydia Wilson had you named Sibley?"

"Yes. But he divorced his second wife and she married again and they adopted me. That's why I'm called Sibley."

Dear God. What was happening to American society as the result of frequent and multiple divorces was horrible to contemplate. With the proliferation of day care centers, Plato's dream was being realized. Children would soon think that all adults were equally their parents, the particular couple who conceived them having long since been lost in the general mass of mankind.

"Can you get me the things I require or shall I employ professional help?"

"Better hire someone, Mr. Cadbury. It's not my sort of thing. So what's the deal between us?"

"I will bill you for such charges as the one I mentioned. For the rest, we will be buccaneers together. It is not uncustomary for there to be an even division of profit in the event of success in such endeavors. I will ask for only twenty-five percent. But let me stress that the sum whose percentages we are discussing may very well turn out to be zero."

William Sibley did not need to know that he was the first new client Amos Cadbury had taken on in fourteen years. Motives seldom bear scrutiny and Amos's were not of the highest. The other lawyers involved in the matter were old adversaries of his. Eugene Wharton had advised Marvin Wilson during the playboy's lifetime; it was not a task Amos had envied him. Wharton's fault was that he had ceased to take his client seriously or perhaps he had imagined that Marvin Wilson, since he had never grown up, would not die. In any case, the will that was languishing in the anteroom of probate was a disgraceful document. Whether or not he could present William Sibley as the sole heir, Amos felt that the young man could expect to get something. Any amount at all would suffice to prove Amos's point about the will. Eugene Wharton himself, like his client, had crossed the great divide. Amos thus did not anticipate gloating if he succeeded. As for Burke, Rusk, Wong & Wagner, they were a firm about which Amos had long had serious doubts. The ostentation of their Chicago offices, their busy involvement in Fox River affairs, from charity to the new sports and entertainment facility near O'Hare—none of this rang true. That they should have been chosen to represent the Las Vegas showgirl who had snared a local millionaire seemed a confirmation. It would not surprise Amos to learn that the firm was a local laundry for ill-gotten money.

Amos did not accompany Sibley through the waiting room. But moments after Sibley was gone, Miss Cleary enterea and began to fuss with the plants. The plants did not need fussing over.

"These notes will acquaint you with some facts about our new client. I should start a file if I were you."

"New client?"

"The case will prove a stimulant, I think."

"What is the nature of the case?"

"A claim of inheritance."

"The name Sibley is not local, is it?"

"The young man is from California. It is his hope to lay his hands on the money Stacey Wilson will not be permitted to have. She cannot inherit on the basis of a crime."

"I'm surprised, Mr. Cadbury."

"So am I."

Had he given way to an ignoble impulse? When young Sibley sauntered into his office, Amos's concern was to come up with a way of getting him out of there quickly. His colleague in Los Angeles had a few debts to call in, but nothing as massive as this. So why? Pride. Vanity. Vindictiveness.

Yes, he decided, all of those. But he would not add to his sins now by going back on his word.

"Get Blanshard on the phone, please."

"Blanshard."

"The private detective. He'll be in the yellow pages."

TWENTY

THE ONLY PACKAGE in the drawer which had been opened was the one containing an alligator purse. Cy took it to a table where he could get some light on it and on the printout of what the drawer contained. Had Elaine consulted the account of what was in the drawer before looking through the drawer itself? Based on her usual efficiency, Cy would have said yes, but she had also brought Tyrone Pajakowski to the Black Museum, thereby dropping in Cy's esteem. Cy drew the task of talking it over with her.

"Talking it over?"

Captain Keegan looked uncomfortable. "Cy, a crime hasn't been committed. We had no written order to keep out of the Black Museum."

"She knew better."

"That's what I want you to find out."

It was difficult to believe that Elaine knew better twelve hours later when Cy took her to the department cafeteria, sat across the table from her and asked her what she had been thinking of when she took Tyrone Pajakowski to the Black Museum.

"Stacey Wilson is his mother."

"You mean he told you she's his mother."

"Are you telling me she isn't? What we were looking for was some kind of proof."

"And he figured that would be in the evidence we gathered to convict his mother."

"So she is his mother?"

"Elaine, cool it. We're on the same side."

"What's the other side?"

"The robbers. We're the cops, right?"

She turned her cup in her saucer. The way she sat, half turned away from him, the fact that she wouldn't meet his eyes, told him how much she wanted this over with. Her problem was that she still wanted to be on Pajakowski's side of the line.

"Tell me how you met him."

"In a supermarket. By accident. He went through the checkout before me."

"An accident."

"That's what it appeared to be."

"Lucky him, huh? Running into someone who works here and can tell him all sorts of things about his mother." Cy leaned forward. "Did it ever occur to you that he's working for his mother, for her lawyers, that the point of all this is to undermine the case we built against her? What did he take out of that drawer?"

That this was his purpose seemed never to have occurred to Elaine. She was speechless. She began to shake her head.

"He took nothing."

"You're sure?"

"You saw him right afterward. You would have known."

"I didn't shake him down, Elaine." He added, "I wanted to."

"I opened the drawer because he specifically wanted to see her purse. He hoped that there would be a photograph, a birth certificate..."

"There are easier ways of obtaining a birth certificate."

"But he wouldn't know."

"Elaine, listen to me. Tyrone Pajakowski ran into you and became friendly with you in order to get into that Black Museum. Are you telling me he went to all that trouble, looked into a purse, and then left?"

"That's exactly what he did."

"I don't believe you. First, I don't believe you're as dumb as you're pretending. Second, I don't believe he just took a peek in the drawer and said let's go."

"I opened the purse so he could see inside."

"What did he take from it?"

"Nothing."

She was lying. "Tyrone was put in a reform school when he was thirteen. He has been in trouble ever since, but only one conviction. A light sentence, because he plea-bargained."

She hadn't known that.

"What you did, Elaine, is take an ex-con whose mother is appealing her conviction to have a look at the evidence we gathered against her. You go ahead and cry. It's something to cry about. If we can't trust you, who are we going to trust?"

She pushed back from the table, sobbing, and he let her go. When she disappeared into the ladies' he went on to his office. The main thing he wanted to do was immunize her against Tyrone Pajakowski.

Before he talked to Tyrone, he stopped at the Black Museum and got out the Wilson evidence. Having emptied it, he held the open purse to the light and looked inside. Nothing. And Tyrone hadn't gotten that good a look at it, if Elaine was telling the truth. Cy stared at the contents of the purse, spread on the table. What the hell had he been after? Had he found it or not?

TYRONE WAS LIVING in a motel that had survived its allotted quarter of a century and now functioned as a kind of horizontal rooming house for laborers and construction workers who spent the week in the area and returned to their families for the weekend. WEEKLY RATES fluttered spasmodically in neon on the standard that had replaced the trademark of the chain which had operated the motel in its first lifespan. Cy had assigned himself the surveillance job that turned up the fact that Tyrone was in unit 7. Lucky seven? The superstition of ex-cons. Why did people whose luck was so uniformly bad retain a mystical interest in Lady Luck?

There was no car at unit 7 but the one at 13 checked out as stolen. Some skills are never forgotten. It had been a stolen car that had put Tyrone in prison. Either he was arrogant or stupid, borrowing transportation after the run-in in the Black Museum. Horvath settled down. He would wait for Tyrone to get into that car and start to drive it. That would give him reason to take him downtown where they could have a nice talk.

Stakeouts brought back the desire to smoke, unless there was a smoker in the car with him. It was the idea, not the reality, of tobacco that Horvath missed. Keegan had told him that Nickles, the guy who drowned himself, had talked to Father Dowling about joining a monastery. Horvath imagined monks sitting all day in church or in their cell, thinking. Well, praying, but it was like thinking. But maybe it was flattering to call what he did sitting here watching Tyrone's unit thinking. Images, disconnected ideas, floated across his mind. The only time he seemed in control of his mind was when he was doing something, or when he was writing a report. Typed out, just about anything began to make sense. The problem with Elaine, he'd said, was that she didn't think of what she was doing. As if that was true only of women. How many people know what the hell they're doing while they're doing it?

When Cy thought of praying it was of reciting the set formulas he had learned as a boy, the acts of faith, hope and charity, the act of contrition. The Our Father, Hail Mary, and Creed. He wished they'd use that creed at Mass. He began to say the act of faith, out loud, feeling like an altar boy. "Because you have revealed them, who can neither deceive nor be deceived." He felt good to get through it the first go, and then he saw the car pull in at unit 7.

Elaine McCorkle got out, slammed the door and then knocked on the motel door. What a forlorn figure she was, standing there. Well, she knew what she was doing now. It was like a slap in the face, seeing her running to Tyrone after their talk in the cafeteria. Cy would have bet he'd gotten through to her. The unit door opened and Elaine stepped inside.

TWENTY-ONE

"THEY KNOW ALL ABOUT YOU," she said, pushing into the room.

"Whoa, there." Tyrone was wearing nothing but underwear shorts and he must still have been in bed, as it was all mussed up.

"Lieutenant Horvath has been checking you out."

"Sweetie, what have I done wrong?"

"You lied to me."

"When was that?"

"You withheld information."

"Elaine, if I have to tell everybody everything I'm guilty every time, right?"

Her eyes made a tour of the squalor in which he lived. Not only was the bed a mess, there were clothes just thrown anywhere. She would have guessed him to be neat, he dressed so well. Along one wall of the room ran a long low shelf that functioned as desk, the top of a chest of drawers, and table for the televison set. She realized that the television set was on. Elaine gaped. She could not believe what she saw on the screen. From the bathroom came the sound of flushing. She turned and surprised in Tyrone's eyes a moment of panic. Then he smiled, the same smile with which he had listened to her when he was Gordon and they had lunch at the Great Wall.

"Thin walls."

And then she noticed that some of the clothes on the floor were women's clothes. My God in heaven, what had she walked into? She turned and started blindly toward the door, but Tyrone got there first and stopped her.

"Elaine, relax. It's just a little R and R, it doesn't mean a thing."

The bathroom door opened and Elaine could not keep herself from turning.

The girl couldn't have been more than seventeen. She wore a bra and panties and had a towel over her shoulders. Her smile was insolent. Elaine felt in the presence of some vast knowledge of which she had none. She refused to look at the bed. The television emitted the sounds of a pig sty. Elaine pushed Tyrone aside and pulled open the door, but it would not open all the way. He had put the chain in place. She tugged at the knob, but of course the door would not open.

"You have to close it first."

When she did he got between her and the door again. "Where are you going?"

What difference did it make? What did he care? The bed jangled as the girl threw herself upon it.

"Who is she, Gordon?"

"Gordon!" Elaine looked at the little scamp. "Is that what he told you his name is?"

"Hey, is this your old lady? You married? He never told me he had a wife."

The thought that she might be married to such a man brought a roar of contempt from Elaine. The girl scrambled off the bed and began to gather up her clothes, keeping a wary eye on Elaine. Her jeans were so tight she had trouble pulling them on. A T-shirt and slip-ons and she was ready to go.

"Turn off that televison," Elaine ordered. She may never have been to bed with a man but she was now in charge. "Let her go," she said to Tyrone.

He removed the chain, opened the door and bowed deeply, but when the girl went out he slapped her on the bottom. "Later, baby."

"Who is that child?"

"Her daddy runs this place."

"You are beneath contempt."

"But not above suspicion."

"Will you put some pants on, please? And clean up this place. I can't stand such a mess."

"Give me a hand."

And she did, God forgive her, picking up and folding and putting away. She even made the bed, as if to draw a veil over what he and that child had been doing there. He lay on the bed, with his hands behind his head and smiled at her.

"So you came here to give me a warning."

She remained standing, leaning against the long shelf. She told him of Lieutenant Horvath's inquisition.

"I've never been so humiliated in my life. Why didn't you tell me your background?"

"The way you're acting right now is the answer to that. You wouldn't have given me the time of day."

"You weren't after the time of day. What were you really looking for in that purse?" That calling card could not have been it. Besides, he had given it to her to put back.

"Trust."

"Don't talk riddles."

"Elaine, you were there. What did we do, glance in the purse. We didn't even look at the rest of the stuff. It was a test."

"A test?"

He swung his legs and put his feet on the floor, looking away from her. "You don't know what it's like, to be on the outside from the time you were a kid. We gôt along so well, but I've learned not to trust people. Where I've been you put people to the test. That's what I was doing with you. Afterward, I could tell you everything."

"You're lying."

He nodded. "Sure I'm lying. Why the hell should you believe me?"

She was totally confused. In the past ten minutes she had been put through such a stream of impressions, an emotional MTV. She had seen things she had never seen, and the fact that a man and a woman went to bed together seemed almost unimportant. What had he called it—recreation? None of this fit at all with her vision of life; it was insane. That she should still be here, talking to this man, was the most incredible thing of all.

There was a knock at the door. Tyrone looked at her.

"The runt. She'll go away."

Indeed she would. What a brazen little monkey. Elaine tore open the door and stared into the impassive face of Lieutenant Cyril Horvath.

TWENTY-TWO

THE HAGERTYS' FLIGHT for Helena did not leave until the following day, so Father Dowling offered to put them up at the rectory, but the thought of a night in a priest's house was too much, so he got them rooms at the O'Hare Inn.

"I'll have someone take you there, but first you have to have one of Marie Murkin's dinners."

Charlotte and Mitch didn't want to offend Marie Murkin, not after the kindness she'd shown them.

"I'm having meat loaf!" Marie wailed, but of course the Hagertys loved meat loaf and Charlotte insisted on helping in the kitchen, while Mitchell stood in the study shaking his head at the shelves of books.

"Smells like it's all right to smoke in here."

"The Cubs are on later."

"Baseball?"

There went that possible way of passing the evening. After dinner, the women stayed in the kitchen and Mitch lit up a cigar Father Dowling gave him. The westerner puffed contemplatively, then looked at the pastor.

"While Charlotte's out there, maybe we could talk about Walter."

"Of course."

"I've got to tell you, no one was more surprised than we were. The way he told it, Walter had the world by the tail."

"I understand he was very successful in what he did."

"Made phone calls."

Roger Dowling let it go. It was unclear whether Mitch thought this a trivial occupation.

"Imagine making a living talking."

"It's done all the time."

Mitch chuckled. "That's no lie. The thing about Walter, he didn't sound like a man who was that down. He was going to visit us in June, been talking about it for months, and this time I think he meant it. If he was sad, that's all he needed, a little Montana and he'd be all right again."

"Had he talked about going back?"

"No. Wouldn't hear of it. Maybe a visit. But he meant it this time, I know he did."

"When did you last talk to him?"

"That's what gets me. Near as I can figure it, it had to be the day he did it. When we got the news, I figured it was an accident. That's what you think when you hear somebody's drowned. They sure he did it?"

Survivors seldom accept that their son, cousin, parent, friend, killed himself. Suicide cannot really be thought—the same person as victim and killer, inside and outside, beginning an action the point of which is the end of all action. As a student Roger Dowling had never trusted philosophers who spoke easily of suicide, as one choice among others. His work as a pastor made him even more skeptical of their easy theories.

"How does a man that size drown himself in a bathtub?"

The question had occurred to everyone on the scene. Hart's conjecture that, given the disposition of the body, Walter had just slid beneath the water, simply restated the problem. But the question how was merely a facet of the question why.

At nine Karen came by in the minibus to take the Hagertys to their airport hotel. Roger Dowling felt half inclined to go along. The minibus had the allure of a ride at the amusement park.

"They're nice people," Marie said after they had left.

"Yes."

"Did you talk to him about you know what?"

"I could hardly avoid it."

"Hagertys had to be Catholics."

So he had misunderstood what for Marie was topic number one. Her missionary sense seemed keener than his own. "I thought you meant the suicide."

"They'll never agree that it was suicide."

"Is that what Charlotte said?"

Marie nodded vigorously, as if that closed the matter.

"She thinks it was an accident."

"It's what she thinks it isn't that matters to her."

THE FOLLOWING DAY Phil Keegan arrived late for the noon mass but came on to the rectory for lunch. He was a very preoccupied man. The drama of Elaine McCorkle continued. Roger Dowling listened to the account of the drama at Tyrone Pajakowski's motel, shaking his head, puffing his pipe. Poor Walter Nickles was dead, prayed over and consigned to the earth, and Elaine went from madness to madness.

"Has anyone talked to Stacey Wilson about all this?"

"It's a delicate matter, Roger. The appeal is based on the court record. It would be difficult to justify interviewing her and I don't want us doing anything that would give the defense a spurious excuse."

"The case will end up being a major local employer."

"I thought we were through with it," Phil said with disgust. "What kind of soup is this, Marie?"

"Soupe aux pois."

"Don't translate it."

"What's that mean?"

"Don't ask."

"Well, aren't we in a sweet mood today?"

"Tell her about Elaine, Roger."

Marie had pulled out a chair and sat before he finished the sentence. "I heard a bit of what you said."

Marie had faced Phil. She wanted this story from the horse's mouth. Roger Dowling found it even sadder the second time.

"Well, I never," Marie said. "And she was here making a novena to St. Anthony just days ago."

"It's the disloyalty," Phil lamented. "Did she break any laws? No. But if that's the most we can say for one another..."

Cy had arrested Tyrone Pajakowski on a charge of auto theft although Elaine insisted that she had driven the car to the motel. But she didn't know which one was the stolen car, because when they came out of the motel, the car was gone. Apparently Tyrone's teenaged lover had driven off in it. It had been recovered, wrecked, and was being combed for evidence of Tyrone. Bail had been set but Tyrone still languished in jail. Elaine had offered to post bail but it was Tyrone who refused freedom on that basis.

"I'd like to have a talk with that girl," Marie said.

"You already did."

"Yes, and if she'd listened to me one man would still be alive, another wouldn't be in jail, and she wouldn't be the laughingstock of the parish."

The parish of St. Hilary's might be Marie's point of reference, but it was doubtful that Elaine McCorkle saw her life in parochial terms.

"She's not local, is she, Phil?"

"She's from Cairo, not the suburb, the city downstate. I met her folks once when they were up on a visit. There's no need for them to know about this but I wonder if they'll hear."

"Elaine certainly won't tell them."

"Did you fire her, Phil?"

"I told her to take her vacation now. We'll talk about it in three weeks."

"You old softie."

"It's all this pea soup I'm having."

TWENTY-THREE

FOR THE FIRST TIME in his life, Tuttle had a sense of what his career would have been like if he had joined a large firm, not that anyone would have hired him when he emerged from six years of law school. Even if they had, the decade it took him before he got by the bar exam would have put him on the street. But this meant that he could appraise the pluses and minuses of the large firm from the perspective of the established loner.

Work space had been set aside for him during his Chicago visits and Melanie Jewel could not have been more helpful. His tapes had suitably impressed everyone that mattered, not least of all Jewel.

"Wheaton's testimony sounds entirely different on your tape," she said. "Do you do much court work?"

"My idea of heaven is arguing before a jury."

"You have a way."

What the tape made clear, the relevant members of the firm agreed, was that Billy Wheaton had seen a figure besides Wilson in the boat before it set sail and that he identified the figure as Mrs. Wilson because of the gear she was wearing. But it was foul-weather gear of the most common kind.

"What kind of cap?" Tuttle had asked. No one else had ever thought of a cap.

"Wool."

"Pulled down tight on the head?"

"Tuttle," Billy said. "That wind was a sonofabitch."

"What we have," said Hasser, "is someone or other helping Wilson before he cast off. Whether that person crewed for him is unknown. Not even Wheaton saw two figures once the boat was under way. If ever a crew would have been visible it would have been while the boat was getting under way."

Accolades all around. Lunch with the big shots in the private dining room. Coffee with Jewel and lesser lights. Tuttle tried to enjoy his success but he had no practice at it. It was with a sense of escape that he went back to his hole in the wall in Fox River, got the old tweed hat settled over his eyes, his feet on the desk, and Peanuts Pianone as his audience. Pizza was on the way.

He was on his second slice of carpaccio when the other angle hit him. If his Wheaton tape got Stacey off the hook, or at least off the boat, the McNaughton tapes left her a liar as to her actual whereabouts.

"What's her secret, Peanuts?"

Peanuts knew a rhetorical question when he heard one. Tuttle had once referred to what he was doing as brainstorming but Peanuts had taken offense. Had he thought it a crack about his limited capacities? In any case, it was a one-sided activity.

"She's not on the boat, she's not at the farm. So much I've established." He paused. In his mind's eye he saw Melanie Jewel concede that with a little nod. "I'm wondering where she was. Not that I care *where,* Peanuts. I had the idea and I let it go. Okay, okay, first things first and one thing at a time and all that, but I want to know *who with.* She's protecting someone, Peanuts. It would have been the easiest thing in the world to say, why, I was looking after Joe those days because he had a bad cold."

"Who's Joe?"

"It could be Pete."

"Who's Pete?"

"The twin of repeat." Tuttle laughed. That had just jumped out of his memory, playground stuff. "Anyone, Peanuts. Some man. We are not talking about a nun here. She does not play the tuba for the Salvation Army. She's been showing nine-tenths of her body in Las Vegas for years. The point is she was with somebody and she's sitting down there in Joliet and running the risk of sitting in some such place all her life because she does not want to name him. Why?"

Peanuts rummaged around in the pizza box, got hold of the last slice, and lifted his single brow. Tuttle nodded. "Go ahead, take it." He took off his hat and twirled it on his index finger, then put the hat back on.

"Because she's scared, Peanuts."

It was there that, given the local reputation of the Pianone family, Tuttle dropped it. Stopped talking out loud about it. But he pursued the spoor and it was with Melanie Jewel that he continued. They took coffee into his workspace and he asked if she'd seen the Al Pacino movies. Okay. So think who runs Las Vegas where Stacy Wilson worked all those years.

"Say during those unaccounted-for days she was with someone like that. Someone she mentions and it's all over for her."

"This is just guessing."

"Was I there? Of course it's guessing."

"No tapes?" She looked at him over her coffee cup like someone playing hide and seek. But she was okay, even in the suit that seemed to be her uniform.

"The key for me is Las Vegas."

Jewel got up and shut the door. He went on.

"You can see what a fix she's in. She's no safer inside than out, any more than keeping quiet so far guarantees anything."

"What are you going to do?"

Here was the difficulty. Tuttle could go to Las Vegas and grow old there without finding out anything. He might say the wrong thing to the wrong person and be worse off than Stacey Wilson.

"The firm has got to pop for an investigator," he said to Melanie.

"To find out if she was there during those days and with whom?" Her eyes seemed to be having difficulty reaching him.

"That will make the appeal a lead-pipe cinch."

"A sure thing?"

"The tapes show where she wasn't. This will show where she was."

"And put her in real danger."

"That has to be taken into account."

Melanie was reluctant to take this idea to Hasser, but Tuttle insisted. He was on a roll. Hasser started to shake his head before Tuttle was really under way.

"Stacey has vetoed any inquiries along those lines."

"You didn't agree to that?"

"It seemed a lot more risky before your tapes, Tuttle. Don't worry, this will more than suffice. No need to embarrass the lady, is there?"

Even Jewel lost interest after that. Tuttle went back to Fox River. He felt that he had already been to Las Vegas and spoken to the wrong people.

TWENTY-FOUR

WHEN PHIL KEEGAN mentioned how delicate a matter it would be for the police to question Stacey Wilson, Roger Dowling was about to suggest that he could drive to Joliet and see what he could see. But he decided that he would make any favor he might do for Phil secondary to a more seemly purpose.

"I'll be seeing Earl when I'm there, Edith. Any message or errand?"

"I just sent him a package. I wish I'd known you were going—he would have gotten it much sooner."

"Well, I'll say hello."

"He's all right as long as he doesn't brood. I think sometimes he thinks he really didn't do what he's in there for, that it was all a mistake, unfair."

"God knows there are plenty running around free who've done worse."

"That's the kind of thing he says."

Father Dowling smiled. "Is he still reading?"

"Till his eyes hang out."

Roger Dowling looked along his shelves for something to lend Earl. Canon law and theology were out, of course, and books in foreign languages. He hesitated over Dorothy Sayers's translation of *The Divine Comedy,* a favorite, but decided against it. Wodehouse, Waugh, James. Trollope. If Earl acquired a taste for Trollope he would not run out of things to read for years. He put *The Eustace Diamonds* in his briefcase but had second thoughts because of the crime in the story, very uncharacteristic of Trollope. Better take *The Warden* in which such crimes as there were were committed by the clergy.

Before leaving he called Jimmy Price the chaplain to tell him he was coming.

"Great. I was going to golf today, but I'll put it off."

Jimmy had been incardinated into Joliet after a quarrel with a previous archbishop who was glad to smooth his way. He liked to say that he had sent Jimmy to Joliet. "I mean the prison." It is said that once a man becomes a bishop he will never again have a bad meal or have the truth spoken to him. Add that he will never tell a joke that doesn't get a laugh. Jimmy considered that he had the last laugh.

"Life is a prison, Roger, did you ever think of that?"

"No."

"We're all doing time, for Original Sin, our own sins. The whole thing is aimed at being released."

"I thought punishment or reward came next."

"Don't spoil my theme. It goes well here."

Jimmy's gray hair was cut short; he was a little jowly now, but his tanned smooth skin made him look younger than he was. He stayed in shape, working out in the prison gym, and jogged around the yard every other morning.

"May your sentence be a long one."

Jimmy had said it on previous visits and he said it again. He loved prison work. "Back to the basics, Roger. Murder, larceny, kidnapping. It's not like little old ladies who wonder if they were mean to their neighbor. With these guys it's the big ones that got them here. Well, maybe they were convicted for something minor, but they've usually done worse than they were arrested for."

Jimmy spoke with real affection. "There comes a point when they stop kidding themselves and blaming others. When that happens, they can accept being here. It's almost like a retreat."

Jimmy's analogies wouldn't travel beyond the prison walls, but they didn't have to. Roger Dowling felt an affinity with the chaplain. Jimmy got Joliet, Roger got Fox River, and they were more content than they had ever been before.

"How's Earl Hospers doing?"

Jimmy shook his head. "Any chance he's innocent?"

"He did what he's here for."

"I wish he could accept that, but he hasn't. You're going to talk with him?"

Roger nodded. "I brought him a book." He showed it to Jimmy.

"A book about a warden! Roger, you've got to be kidding."

It had never occurred to him. And he had set aside *The Eustache Diamonds* lest in some way he offend Earl.

"I'll explain it to him."

"I'd like to be there when you do."

"While I'm seeing him, could you do me a favor?"

"*Sed tantum dic verbo.*"

"Check to see who's been to visit Stacey Wilson since she got here?"

"Stacey Wilson. Oh, that's right, she's Fox River. Is she a parishioner?"

"Hardly. My parishioners are little old ladies who wonder if they've been mean to their neighbors. It's just curiosity."

"I'll see what I can do."

How little Earl had changed during the time he had been here. It was a somber thought that he would grow old, and Edith and his children would as well, before he got out.

"I don't want you to misunderstand the title, Earl." He got out the Trollope.

There were many times when Roger Dowling felt inadequate as a priest, but his half hour with Earl Hospers was the worst in a long while. *I was in prison and you visited me.* But what was he supposed to say to the man? Your wife is doing well and so are your kids? Any good news might be bad news to Earl, things he could not himself take part in. But it was Earl who finally got him off the hook.

"I'm not the only Fox River rat here, not since Stacey Wilson was put over in the women's wing."

"How does news get around here?"

Silly question, with all the radios and TVs in evidence, but it gave Earl a topic and he became engrossed in describing prison life, speaking as if he were an observer of it.

"Father Price is a good man, Earl."

He nodded. "I go to Mass, if that's what you're after."

"I'm glad to hear it."

Earl looked away. "How's Edith?"

"If I'd given her more warning she might have come."

"Having visitors is the worst part, Father Dowling."

"I can understand that."

"And not seeing the kids."

He wanted to tell Earl his sons and daughter were doing well, and they were, but it seemed unfair knowing more about a man's children than he did.

"I'm writing to Joey. We play chess. A very slow match, but I just learned how."

A neutral mode of communication, but communication nonetheless. Did he write to Edith?

"HOW LONG DO YOU SUPPOSE they'll keep Earl Hospers here, Jimmy?" he asked the chaplain later.

"He should be eligible for parole in a decade or so. Here's the Wilson visiting list."

He looked at it then and there. There was no entry for Tyrone Pajakowski.

"Have you talked with her, Jimmy?"

"Just said hello. She didn't know whether she was a Christian, let alone Catholic."

"I'd like to see her."

Jimmy reached for his phone. "Any particular reason?"

"About her son."

"That ought to do it."

Jimmy took him to the vistors' room on the women's side and the collar absolved him of the need of talking to her through a grille. Roger Dowling was surprised how tall Stacey was when she stood in the doorway of the room. Jimmy introduced him and then withdrew. Roger Dowling had stood to take her hand and now they sat on either side of a little table.

"I think this is the first time I've been out of sight of a guard since I was brought here."

Her pale blue dress did not seem like prison garb and there were sequins on the white pullover.

"Tyrone Pajakowski says he's your son."

"He told you that?"

He shook his head. "No, the police did. First a girl and then the police. The girl works for Captain Keegan and Tyrone persuaded her to take him where the evidence for your case is kept."

"That's my fault."

"Oh?"

"It's a long story. Anyway, it was a mistake. My lawyers are certain now my appeal will get me acquitted."

"Did you kill your husband?"

She smiled. "Do you know how many times I've been asked that?"

He waited.

"You figure I wouldn't lie to a priest?"

"Would you?"

She made a little cross on her breast. "Cross my heart and hope to die. I wasn't even in Fox River when it happened."

"Not at the farm?"

"I only said that because I thought it wouldn't matter where I said I was. Then that drunk claimed to have seen me on the boat and I was stuck with it." She stopped and wrinkled her nose. "Get a load of me, talking my head off. My lawyers advised me to talk to no one." She peered at him. "You are a priest, aren't you?"

"Would I lie to a laywoman? Yes, I'm a priest."

"I figured the other one wouldn't trick me."

"No. Stacy, if you were somewhere else and you could prove it, why in heaven's name didn't you speak up?"

"That's my secret."

"Some secret, if you'd spend the rest of your life in prison for something you didn't do."

"It sounds dumb, I suppose. It isn't."

"Are you afraid of someone?"

"Me afraid?"

"Are you protecting someone?"

"It's no use, Father. Besides it doesn't matter. I'm not staying. Maybe if I were..."

"Why hasn't Tyrone come to see you?"

"That's not important. Father, would you talk to him? The way he was raised he was bound to get in trouble, and I take the blame for that but I had no authority with him. Why should he listen to the mother who hadn't even bothered to raise him?"

"He might listen to you now."

Her eyes took on a vacant expression. "Talk to him. Please."

TWENTY-FIVE

COULD A MOTHER wonder if her child was her own? Stacey sometimes thought she knew what it was like when a guy doubted he was the father of a woman's baby. It could have been anyone and, in the Age of Aquarius, it might be. But she had felt Tyrone form within her, counted the days, and not because she was looking forward to having her baby. She wanted the discomfort to be over, to lose weight, to be young again. She wasn't yet seventeen when he was born, nine months to the day since she had waved Pajakowski off at San Diego. They had been married downtown by a judge who took no interest in them at all, a raw seaman and his teenage bride. They had spent three days in the sack.

The baby came, a boy, and she named it Tyrone after Tyrone Power. By then Jock was dead, pitched by a rolling sea into the propeller of a fighter plane warming up on deck, buried at sea. The only picture she had of him was a strip from a booth where they had taken turns making faces at the camera. There was one of them kissing. Two kids. She was a mother, a war widow, beneficiary of his GI insurance.

She got out of Dago for fear she'd do it again, marry some other swab, have another kid... The future? She was too young to think of the future. She moved to Vegas, roomed with two other girls whose advice about Tyrone she took. Put him in a foster home. She did. It was almost too easy. Mrs. Plaisance, the woman who took him in, already had a house full of kids—the old woman who lived in a shoe—and she loved it. She let Stacey come by and see Tyrone and at first she did. It hurt a lot when she realized he didn't know her from Eve. It seemed better all around to keep out of the way.

Besides, she had been swept into the excitement of Vegas. Her body had improved from having the baby, there was more of her and it was in the right places, and she had a good sense of rhythm. Darlene coached her and the next thing you know she was on the line with Darlene. Their roommate, Gloria, was too short. She began to pick up guys and bring them to the apartment while Stacey and Darlene were working.

"You're a hooker," Darlene said, the first time they interrupted Gloria at her trade.

"So?"

Darlene looked at Stacey, and the shock left her face. She shrugged. "So get yourself another apartment."

They parted friends. A good thing. A year later, Darlene too was working the casinos for johns. Stacey did it, but not for money. For money she got a job in the Monte Carlo, first watching machines, then dealing blackjack, but she didn't have the gift so she became a waitress. Long before that happened, she had watched her two friends sink, sliding down the scale until they weren't even let into the casinos anymore and had to look for trade in the little places on the fringes of the Strip. Darlene took an overdose on her twenty-eighth birthday. She looked forty. By that time, Stacey hadn't seen Gloria for years. The urn of Darlene's ashes was shipped to Pennsylvania. It made you think.

She reclaimed Tyrone, took a place on the far side of town from the Strip, decided to live a normal life. But Tyrone wasn't used to her—he was four years old—and she sure as hell wasn't used to him. The way he watched her was unsettling. She would be watching TV and become aware of him and turn, and sure enough he might be sitting sideways on a chair, one foot touching the floor, the other twisted in the rungs, head resting in his hand. He acted as if she had kidnapped him.

She went on working and sometimes she thought she worked to earn money to pay the babysitters so she could go to work. The thought of just staying home all day with Tyrone sent a chill through her. Maybe if she had started off doing that, maybe if they knew one another. Did he look like her or Jock? She studied the strip of film and couldn't decide. Maybe he wasn't hers. But that was stupid.

"It's no picnic," Mrs. Plaisance said, happy to have Tyrone back. Tyrone was too big to hold but he pushed the other kids hanging on the woman's skirt away and pressed against her. She ran her hand absentmindedly through his hair, nodding through the long explanation Stacey felt she owed herself at least as to why she was doing this.

"I'm thinking of him. Living with me just isn't good for him."

"Honey, it's all right. I'm glad to have him back."

It became a matter of principle to see Tyrone at least once a week. Mrs. Plaisance showed no particular surprise when Stacey told her she was going to tell Tyrone she was his sister, not his mother. It got so she almost believed that. When she started with Ron Pucceto, a croupier, unhappily married, what else, she had to tell him she didn't want to hear about his goddamn wife or kids.

"I know about them, okay. They're your problem. Do I bend you ear about my little brother?"

"What little brother?"

"See, you didn't even know."

When he wasn't bitching about his life at home, his way of justifying their time together, Ron was all right. Very all right. After several months, Stacey began to wish he didn't have that family. Divorce?

"What's the point?" she asked.

He had a way of moving his fingers around in the mat of hair on his chest, as if he were looking for something. "This isn't fair to you."

"What's fair?"

"Yeah."

It helped to think they were taking some kind of revenge on a cruel world. He was good in bed, no athlete, just tender, patient and considerate. No funny stuff. He became a habit. Stacey didn't know what love was. She didn't want to know. Things were okay just as they were, she didn't mind. Any thought of becoming like the wife he couldn't shut up about or babysitter to a bunch of kids—she'd be like Mrs. Plaisance looking after Tyrone and all the others—repelled her. What she and Ron had was what it was, not all that usual. Other girls said it had to give way to something else or stop but it didn't. Not for years. Not until Marvin Wilson came along.

She lived her life on the Strip, among people like herself, the crooks who ran the show, and the plane-loads of suckers who arrived on the hour, were driven to the casinos, fed, liquored, and parted from the cash they'd brought along. They kept coming back, that was the funny part. Not that she recognized them, but a guy would bend her ear about last spring, or remember February?—questions she didn't have to answer—a smile was enough. Why did they come back? Not for her, not for the glitz.

"They come to lose," Ron said.

"That don't make any sense."

"Doesn't."

"That's what I said. Who wants to lose?"

He pinched her in the big dip between her rib cage and the flare of her hip. It was only later that night, unable to sleep, that she wondered if he'd been telling her she was the same. A loser.

She was always figuring things out too late. Like when she realized that they let Ron go on with her because it was only what it was and would never be anything else. He belonged to two families, she finally realized, and neither one allowed divorce. Her main reaction to this was a sense of security. Ron meant protection of a necessary sort.

No one stayed for long, except the employees of the casinos, those dealing or running a crap game, not waitresses, not entertainers. From time to time, a croupier would try to beat the house, work with one of the players. Where did guys like that go after they were caught?

"Don't ask," Ron said.

"I just did."

"I didn't hear you."

So she ran her hand through his chest hair and shut up. Geez. And then Marvin Wilson came on the scene. Stacey was swept off her feet, no doubt about that. He was the first guy she had known who had real money and wasn't a crook. Even so when they married in the James Dean Marriage Chapel it had seemed less real than the civil ceremony in San Diego years before. The first weeks of her marriage she spent not taking calls from Ron but finally she spoke to him.

"Why?"

She didn't feel she owed him an explanation. Life with Marvin was okay, she had no complaints. "Why what?"

"If you wanted to get married you should have told me. I'll marry you."

"Your wife might object. And my husband."

"Husband. That's a joke."

Ron's plan was that he would get a divorce and she would get a divorce and then they would marry and live happily ever after in Vegas. Maybe he meant it. But they wouldn't let him. He told her as if it would break her heart.

"Won't let you?"

"I want to end up dead I file for divorce."

"You Catholics."

"That has nothing to do with it."

"What they? Who's they?"

"Don't ask."

Stacey had spent her years in Vegas trying not to know too much about those who ran the Strip. Ron's new idea was that she should divorce Marvin and come back to him. The way it had been. She didn't tell him to go to hell because she was already worried that Marvin was tiring of her. And then she got the phone call from Tyrone.

"Where're you calling from?" The thought that he might show up at the door made her jumpy. She hadn't told Marvin about Tyrone.

He was working in a grain elevator, out on parole. She sent him money. She agreed to see him when he got out and suggested the yacht club. She had not been prepared for the emotions that swept over her at the sight of her son, now a young man. How much like

Jock he looked. When she thought of the kind of mother she had been to him, she wanted to cry. Here she was a wealthy woman and Tyrone had nothing but what he had walked around with.

"If you insist on having a gigolo please do not parade him around the yacht club." Marvin smiled but it was like a denture in a glass of ice water.

"Gigolo?"

"Good-looking younger-than-you male. Paid escort."

He meant Tyrone. She was both mad and wanted to laugh, but she was damned if she would give him any explanation. She did tell Tyrone and for a moment wished she hadn't, the way he looked her over.

"Get rid of the sonofabitch."

"Did you ever hear to the golden goose?"

"I've given it."

"Besides he may get rid of me first. I'll get a good lawyer."

"You'd do better as his widow."

She laughed. Marvin spent half his life looking after his health, having tests taken, going into Mayo or whatever for a complete and total checkup. The verdict that he was in great shape reassured him for a day or two and then his worries began again.

"He'll live to be a hundred."

When Tyrone suggested that she hasten Marvin on his way, it might have been a joke, the kind of chatter he'd whiled away his time in prison with. But the suggestion had first been Ron's, and the way Ron said it made it clear he saw it as a job that could easily be done. He wanted her back, but how badly? Stacey liked the status of wife and Ron could never give her that. 'They' wouldn't let him. She almost told Tyrone that if she wanted to get rid of Marvin she knew experts at that sort of thing. But Ron's buttoned lip was contagious; there were things you didn't say.

Tyrone's remark that Marvin could afford lawyers that would make any she could afford look sick worried her. He was right. If they parted on a sour note. The conversation with Tyrone got her thinking and she went off to Vegas to talk with Ron. No need to spell it out in black and white. Ron would know how these things were done and would be happy to arrange it so things would be the way they had been, only better. One morning he shook her awake and pointed at the television. She had become a widow. Ron was already out of bed, scrambling into his clothes. Being careful.

"Ron?"

He looked at her. "Don't ask."

Stacey tried to think of it as an act of God. She was being looked after by a benign providence as she flew home to Chicago. The representative of the airline gave her a message when she got off the plane. Inside the envelope was a number. Assuming it was Ron, she stopped at a phone on the way to the baggage area. Tyrone answered.

"Congratulations."

"That's pretty cold-hearted."

"You can thank me later."

Click. It was when she was watching the carousel go by, waiting for her bags, that she figured out what he meant. The little bastard, trying to take credit for it. Who was he trying to kid? What a con.

TWENTY-SIX

"WHO'S HE?" Edith asked Karen, indicating the young man marveling at the minibus.

"I don't know." Karen's voice was musical as she stepped back from the window so she could observe without being observed.

"Tell him it's not for sale."

"You tell him."

"He's not my type."

Karen professed to be shocked at such a remark from Edith, but a few minutes later Edith looked out and saw Karen in conversation with the stranger. She tugged at her sweatshirt, tossed her head to get her long hair out of her eyes, seemed to be laughing a lot. Edith decided to go out and find out who he was.

"Gordon Koppens, ma'am. I'm admiring this vehicle."

"It's been a great help."

"In what way?"

Now that Edith was there he ignored Karen completely, concentrating on the older woman, but Edith had the sense that his whole performance was for Karen's benefit. He was fascinated to learn of the way the school was being used and duly impressed that Edith was in charge.

"Karen's a volunteer."

"You haven't told me your name."

What a charmer. Still, it felt good to have the boy pretend that she was still competition for someone like Karen.

"Edith," he repeated. "I have an Aunt Edith. Much older than you, of course."

"Are you in the parish?"

"I'm thinking about it."

"That's the rectory over there. The pastor's name is Father Dowling."

"I won't rush into it. A man shouldn't change parishes just like that."

"What is your parish?"

"It's in Nevada."

He was new in town and just passing by when he saw the minibus and he was glad they'd taken the trouble to come out and talk.

"Take him for a ride in it, Karen."

The suggestion was meant to remind herself not to respond to this young man's flattery. Karen could take care of herself, Edith was sure of it. What possible harm could there be in taking Gordon Koppens for a spin in the minibus in the middle of the day?

Back in her office Edith felt suddenly overwhelmed by loneliness. Father Dowling had brought reassuring news of Earl, but it only served to underscore the lonely years that still lay ahead of her. She dared not even think of parole. Earl told her the first request was almost always turned down, but even if it weren't, it could be years off.

The bold young Gordon had made her conscious of how much she missed Earl. How good it would be to have someone to lean on again, someone to shoulder responsibilities. Everything rested on her now and she could handle it, she had proved that, but it was so difficult and lonely. A lump formed in her throat, pity for a still young woman without a man.

But she did not envy Karen. One day, perhaps as accidentally as this encounter with Gordon, Karen would meet a man and it would lead on to marriage, and what a lottery that was. Earl had been the one for her, she had been sure of it the first time they met. They had gone together and then there was a big big wedding, her folks going all out for their only daughter. Had she any premonitions that day of what lay ahead? Of course not. Does any bride when she stands at the altar have any notion that the future may be as bad as the wedding ceremony suggests? And what then? She could have bailed out on Earl after his conviction, let a decent interval go by and then filed for a divorce. Not the Catholic thing to do, though it wasn't unheard of. Maybe she could ask for an annulment. An annulment! After three kids? But Marie Murkin, butting in as usual, just talking generalities of course, assured her that stranger things had happened. Then Edith could have married again. But what assurance would she have that she was not getting into something worse? Oh, the next time she would be more careful, she would... What?

It wouldn't be this stranger, of course, but Karen was at that fateful age when such decisions are made. What moments before had seemed carefree, the foot-loose freedom of youth, now loomed as a mysterious crossroads beyond which anything might lie.

Edith made an impatient noise and pushed back from her desk. Ye gods, she was babbling away to herself like Marie Murkin. But as she strode down the hall toward the murmur of elderly voices she bet herself that no young man would waste his time flattering Marie Murkin when Karen was in the vicinity.

TWENTY-SEVEN

WHEN AMOS CADBURY told Father Dowling that he was representing the adopted child of the divorced and now deceased first wife of Marvin Wilson, the pastor of St. Hilary's seemed unsure whether or not to smile. Amos now had in his possession the birth certificate of William Sibley, his mother's marriage certificates to Wilson and then Sibley, as well as the adoption papers.

"She was the wife before Virginia?"

"You knew the second wife."

"I gave her instructions."

Amos looked around the priest's study, a room full of books and redolent of tobacco. Once Amos had smoked cigars, in moderation, as he had thought, but his physician had persuaded him that this was a pleasure he must forgo. How could one justify a life-threatening habit? The ethics of the decision had seemed compelling. He wondered how Father Dowling had resolved the matter in favor of continuing to smoke. Amos wished he had sought pastoral counsel as well as medical advice. He held in his long fingers the unlit cigar he had taken from the box Father Dowling extended to him. It was Amos's habit to enjoy the tactile and olfactory sensations associated with smoking and Father Dowling indulged him while disapproving of such moral gymnastics. ("Lead us not into temptation, Amos. The prayer is idle if we put ourselves in the way of danger.")

"Did she enter the Church?"

"No. Her interest began as a way of annoying her husband, became genuine, but she never received the grace of conversion."

"Or did not accept it?"

Father Dowling tipped his head noncommittally. "Did you know Virginia?"

"No. Father, I took on young Sibley as a client because in the circumstances his claim was not devoid of merit. There is Virginia, of course, childless. And there is William Sibley. Two claimants, on the supposition that Stacey Wilson was definitively out of the picture as one who could not gain by the murder she was convicted of committing. The appeal seemed routine, another pointless demand on the legal system, justifiable only abstractly."

Father Dowling puffed patiently on his pipe. The force of the past tenses had not escaped him.

"There now seem good prospects that her lawyers will get the conviction overturned."

"Really?"

"The case against her was twofold. She was reported seen on the boat which carried Marvin Wilson to his death. She lied about where she was at the time. The combination convicted her. The defense now has a tape of an interview with the supposed eyewitness of her presence on the boat which allegedly weakens his earlier testimony."

"She was not on the boat?"

"The proof of it is lacking, at any rate."

"But where was she during the time she claims she was at the farm?"

The cigar now seemed simply an odd object he held. "She needn't prove her innocence, Father Dowling. In law, we all get the benefit of the doubt."

"Do you think she's innocent?"

WHILE ALMOST ANYONE can fancy someone else dead, it was Amos Cadbury's experience that nothing short of overwhelming passion can transmute the ordinary man or woman into a killer. Fear, anger. A threat to something passionately wanted, money, love. Given the status he now had in the case, Amos Cadbury had interviewed Stacey Wilson.

This was a task he would normally have left to a subordinate, but in this matter everything depended on his sense of what the woman might or might not have done. A counselor's visiting room in prison is not a setting in which Stacey could manifestly be herself. In any case, she was a person outside Amos's experience. That so young a woman had been married a first time so many years ago was almost startling in its implausibility. But she had been sixteen at the time. Even in the plain toggery of the prison, there was a physical abundance about the woman that Amos, in his seventies, a man of strict and comfortable chastity, a willing celibate since the death of his wife, could not ignore. And she clearly addressed him as a male. Her smile, the way she leaned toward him, the slow confidential tone in which she spoke, gave Amos the sense that he was keeping an assignation rather than an appointment. It was strangely exciting. Reviewing the case, he had thought Marvin Wilson a fool for marrying a Las Vegas showgirl in the early hours of the morning. Seated across from Stacey, he found such folly less implausible.

On the physical level, that is. Talking with Stacey was not an intellectual treat, and while he felt she was being forthright with him, nothing like a sense of the person concealed in that impressive envelope of flesh came through. She had no idea who William Sibley might be.

"He is the adopted son of Marvin Wilson's first wife."

"She still alive?"

"No. Only Virginia is. The next wife."

"I've never met her."

It was unlikely that she would. The instructions she had received from Father Dowling had not taken immediately, but now Virginia lived as an extern sister in a contemplative convent in South Carolina.

"She's a nun."

Smoke was expelled with her laughter. "Are you serious?"

"Quite."

Her smile faded but her eyes remained fixed on his, looking for some clue that it was a joke after all. She shook her head slowly. "I guess that doesn't really surprise me. He could have driven me into the convent too."

"Or into murder."

"I didn't kill him."

"Where were you when he was killed?"

The smile returned. "It's where I wasn't that matters."

"That's true. Had you and Marvin Wilson planned to have children?"

"No!"

"Surely you are still of childbearing age."

His role permitted him to pry and pose preposterous questions. Stacey obviously welcomed the allusion to her youth and presumed fecundity.

"And men, apparently, can sire offspring at an extremely advanced age."

Her head tipped to one side and a glint came into her eye. Good heavens. She thought Amos was referring to himself, sitting here thumping his chest, boasting of his still procreative powers.

"But Marvin had never had children. Perhaps he was impotent?"

"I never asked."

"But then you married in haste, didn't you?"

"We didn't marry in order to have a family."

Could all those teeth possibly be hers? Her smooth skin, abundant hair, as well as the teeth seemed unreal, products of art rather than nature. Amos was completely fascinated by this woman.

"And you are capable of bearing children still?"

"I'm not going to find out."

"You never had any children?"

In any interview there is a point that divides what went before from what follows, a caesura of sorts. Her reaction was difficult to describe. Were Amos to attempt to tell Father Dowling why he considered Stacey's reaction to her possible motherhood odd he would fail. But he knew with the instinct of a lawyer that he had touched on a crucial point.

"Did you ever have a child?"

She sat looking at him impassively.

"By your first husband perhaps?"

"We were married for three days."

"That doesn't answer my question."

"I was sixteen."

"And now you are, what?"

"It's a matter of public record."

"I didn't look it up."

She smiled. She might have been twenty-nine, even in this light.

The rest of the visit was denouement. He outlined for her his precise interest in the case. He represented William Sibley, whose claim would dissolve if her sentence were reversed. She must understand that there was nothing hostile in his client's mind. Sibley's was a case predicated on a contingency which, he could tell her quite sincerely, he doubted now would be realized. As an officer of the court he could not wish anyone to be punished for a crime she had not committed.

"You're sweet."

On the drive back to Fox River, Amos had ample opportunity to contemplate the contingency of his rectitude. He had never met such a woman before, had never before felt the susceptibility to such obvious charms. How vulnerable the seemingly solid structure of his character was. His step, when he swung through the lobby of his building, was quicker than usual and his posture even more perpendicular. Stacey Wilson had conferred gender on him again, and he didn't mind a bit.

The first thing he did was dispatch Blanshard, the investigator he had employed to gather the marriage and birth and adoption papers, to San Diego. Blanshard was back in three days with photocopies. Pajakowski. No triumph there. Odd that the name of the first husband as well as the brevity of the marriage had not come out in the trial. The prosecution had made it seem like a torrid date rather than a marriage. The other photocopy was what Amos had wanted. A son had been born to Stacey Pajakowski in the naval hospital in San Diego not quite nine months to the day after the marriage.

"Did he survive?"

Blanshard kneaded one cheek with a very large hand. "That may take longer. My suggestion is to check out Vegas."

"Do so."

"I have a man there already. I'm going out myself."

"Good."

Thus it was that Amos learned of the son. An ancient Mrs. Plaisance of intermittent clarity of mind had assured Blanshard that Stacey had a son. "How you gonna forget a name like that?" She meant Pajakowski. "He was a mean little fella. Bad streak in him. There are kids like that."

But Blanshard had returned with something else, seeming proof of Stacey Wilson's alibi. Though if true this destroyed Sibley's claim, Amos rejoiced at Blanshard's information that Stacey was seen in Vegas during those days when her husband was adrift on Lake Michigan.

"Why on earth didn't she bring this forward at the trial?"

"I don't think she was free to."

The suggestion that Stacey was saving someone's good name even at the risk of life imprisonment made no sense. But Blanshard went on. The source of his information would deny ever telling Blanshard such a thing. Stacey, it emerged, had had a long-term relationship with a man involved in the shadier side of Nevada activities, married both to his wife and to his associates, unable to sever ties with either. For him to get linked with a murder case in Illinois would be a death sentence, something he would take strenuous measures to prevent happening.

"Could this shadowy admirer of Mrs. Wilson be responsible for Mr. Wilson's death?"

Blanshard shrugged.

"Would he have left his beloved to pay the price for such a thing?"

Amos had the sense that he had reached the outer limit of the investigator's curiosity. If Stacey had proposed using her Las Vegas alibi, she would have endangered her life. That was Blanshard's point. If her lover had come to her rescue, he would have endangered his. But the simple truth was that Amos now had strong reason to believe that Stacey had not killed Marvin Wilson, that she had been wrongly found guilty and was very likely to be freed when the revised version of Billy Wheaton's testimony was heard. No need to establish where she had actually been.

"I have asked my man to continue looking into the matter of her son." Thus Amos concluded his account of these matters in the rectory of St. Hilary's.

"She is a remarkable woman," Father Dowling said. "Of the earth earthy."

"Yes."

"She reminds me of one of those women who show up in the Gospels, with whom Christ converses. Women with unusual backgrounds, multiple husbands, a bit shunned by others. They nonetheless come through most sympathetically."

"Mary Magdalene?" Amos thought that was going too far.

"The woman at the well."

"Ah." He reserved judgment. He would look it up. "How old would the son be, Amos?"

"In his twenties. Isn't that amazing?"

"He would have a far stronger claim than your client, wouldn't he?"

"Of course."

TWENTY-EIGHT

"MRS. MURKIN?"

"Yes."

"Can we talk?"

Interrupted as she was preparing the May altar, Marie was both surprised and wary to turn and see the substantial figure of Elaine McCorkle. But the expression on the woman's face was not belligerent. Marie would not soon forget Elaine's reaction to her interpretation of the novena the young woman had been making to St. Anthony. Much less would she forget the scolding she'd had to endure from Father Dowling on that occasion. An occasion when she had been at fault, she admitted that. Indeed, having admitted it once, she had been willing to admit it again and again, while pointing out that what Father Dowling called her nosiness others might call womanly concern, even a pastoral impulse.

"Just don't let it happen again," the pastor had said, finding her extenuating remarks unwelcome. Was she letting it happen again now, leading Elaine out of the church, on the far side, away from the rectory? Not at all. Elaine had come to her. And with an apology for the previous episode!

"I see now you were just being kind."

"Elaine, it's my job." How sweet a vindication. Marie wished now she had taken Elaine to the rectory. She began to walk her around the church now. "Come have a cup of tea."

"I was caught up in a false relationship."

Marie sighed, as if her own life had been marked by ambiguous affairs.

"I suppose I was trying to get God on my side. You know. What I'm doing is wrong but He understands, so it's really okay?"

A most astute observation. Elaine had learned from her experience, there was no doubt of that. They settled down at the kitchen table with the hall door closed and enjoyed a good cup of tea.

"It was humiliating, being called on the carpet by Captain Keegan. Of course he was absolutely right."

"Are things better now?"

"Mrs. Murkin, it's poor Walter I think of."

A hush fell over the kitchen. Marie realized she was in the presence of a woman whose indifference had caused a man to kill himself. To call this prestige might seem callous, but it undoubtedly contributed to Elaine's interest. It seemed to melt pounds from her, rearrange her hair, firm the shape of her face, put the glint of tragedy in her eyes. Marie put her hand on the young woman's, much as pilgrims touch the toe of St. Peter's statue in Rome. And after all Elaine had been through, she thought of Walter. For years a veiled mysterious woman had visited the grave of Rudolph Valentino on the anniversary of his death, leaving a rose, then hurrying off into obscurity. What woman had not envied that disconsolate figure? Not at all a farfetched analogy, as soon became clear.

"I may never marry now, Mrs. Murkin. I want my life to be a tribute to Walter, to what he felt for me."

Functioning as Phil Keegan's secretary did not seem an appropriate expression of this wish.

Elaine added, "I read that one of Marvin Wilson's wives ended up in the convent, sort of."

Marie became immobile. She would never say a word against the religious vocation, but like most women she had an instinctively negative reaction to it. The skies would open and a thunderbolt seek her out if in the rectory kitchen of St. Hilary's she had told Elaine to get rid of such thoughts. Thank God it was not as bad as that.

"Working for the police department?" Elaine shook her head. "I've already given notice. What I want is meaningful work, something humble but important, something I can dedicate to Walter."

Marie thought Elaine might well be describing her own job. Or Edith Hospers's. Was that the whir of the wings of the Holy Spirit she heard? It seemed an inspiration.

"Perhaps you could work here, Elaine. At the parish center. It's starvation wages, of course."

"I don't care."

And Marie could see in the girl's eyes the romantic determination to subsist on simple foods, to rise early and retire late and in between to give herself for others, permitting from time to time a little moisture in the eye as she thought of Walter.

"Let me see what I can do."

Elaine looked around. "How I envy you, devoting yourself to the parish, this house, the pastor."

The picture of herself as self-effacing had its charms but Marie found them to be limited. Should she perhaps underscore the responsibilities of her position, the delicacy involved in being the power behind the throne?

"I'll see what I can do."

TWENTY-NINE

TUTTLE WHOOSHED UP in the elevator but when he came into the reception area and started toward the hallway that would take him to the workspace that had been assigned him, the receptionist called out to him.

"Mr. Butler?"

"Tuttle."

She consulted a sheet, nodded. "Tuttle. Right. This is for you."

He took the manila envelope and started away. "You're to open it here."

Tuttle didn't like it, but what could he do? He opened the envelope. Inside was a smaller envelope containing a check and a letter from Hasser thanking him for his consultation. The kiss-off. Tuttle opened the smaller envelope and read the amount of the check. He blinked and read it again. The gratification he felt carried him back to the elevator and down to street level. Only when he had settled behind the wheel of his Toyota did the resentment begin. The check represented the largest amount Tuttle had seen on a check meant for him since he had started practice. It would get his more persistent creditors off his back. He could afford a secretary again, if only on a day-by-day basis. His ship had come in. But there was a fleet approaching harbor and why should he settle for this?

He got out of the car, went back into the lobby and telephoned Melanie Jewel. "Tuttle. Let me buy you a cup of coffee."

"Where are you?"

"In the lobby."

"I heard you weren't with us anymore."

"A farewell cup."

"I'll be right down."

She was a pal, no doubt of that, girlish despite the pinstripe suit and pink blouse, smiling as she came toward him across the lobby. Tuttle felt an impulse to turn around and see if there wasn't someone behind him she was smiling at.

"I was feeling bad because I hadn't said goodbye."

"When did you hear?"

Hasser had told her that morning.

"Were you surprised?"

She was now. "Why?"

It was nuts to suppose she'd think he'd been treated badly just because the arrangement had come to an end. Hasser thought he had the appeal wrapped so why not cut expenses? He had bought and paid for the tapes—that would be his attitude.

"I'd like to say goodbye to him."

"He left for Las Vegas an hour ago."

"It's been nice working with you, Melanie."

Tuttle shook her hand when they parted in the lobby and drove back to Fox River. After depositing the check, he sat in his locked office, feet on the desk, tweed hat pulled over his eyes and thought. He should feel on top of the world. He had hit big. But he felt disappointment, a letdown.

When he interviewed Billy Wheaton and the McNaughtons, he had assumed the tapes would help Stacey Wilson get off. But it would be a technical victory. Chances are she was guilty as charged. Now, when it seemed more than likely that she was innocent, there were two avenues inviting speculation. One concerned where Stacey had been during those fateful days. The other concerned the death of Marvin Wilson. He had been killed. If Stacey hadn't done it, who had?

He was jarred out of his meditation by a knock on the door. He waited. Another knock. Peanuts. He got to his feet to let him in. Two heads are better than one. Well, one and a half.

Peanuts smiled over an armload of pizza boxes. A six-pack of Pepsi dangled from his hand. He shoved his burden at Tuttle, who was happy to help. Minutes later the two old friends were feeding great wedges of pizza into their mouths, groaning with ecstasy. Good old Peanuts.

"Free," Peanuts said.

"Hmmm?"

"Coupons. I saved them up."

A bonus meal. He almost told Peanuts how he had struck it rich with the Chicago firm, but there was still the lingering note of having been used, of not having taken them for all he could have.

After they had had their fill, Tuttle was in the mood for a nap. The sleep of the just—or of the just fed. But Peanuts shook his head.

"I'm on duty."

"When aren't you?"

Peanuts liked that. The intrepid lawman, ever at the call of a vulnerable citizenry. Peanuts felt that he should be in the patrol car, within reach by radio. Would anything short of Armageddon bring Peanuts to the top of any list of units to call?

Tuttle settled into the passenger seat. The radio went on with the motor. A mesh screen separated front seat from back, a dog sometimes accompanying the officer.

"Anyone in back?"

"Agnes Lamb."

Peanut's nemesis, the black officer who had swiftly moved from being Peanuts's partner to the detective branch, working with Keegan and Horvath. The back seat was empty, of course. Peanuts's postprandial content had been broken by the thought of Agnes because of an item on the radio. Not the police radio. Tuttle switched bands to WBBM and the usual babble of traffic and temperature and snippets of national and global news volleyed back and forth between a male and female announcer. Hurricanes, earthquakes, an outbreak of salmonella, a gangland killing in Las Vegas and, locally, a breakneck pursuit by police of a stolen vehicle that had ended in a spectacular crash of the pursued vehicle. Which was empty by the time the pursuing officer got to it. And then the unmistakable voice of Agnes Lamb.

"The speed was in excess of eighty at times."

"How did he get away?"

"'The driver,'" Agnes corrected.

"You think it was a woman?"

"No. But I don't think it wasn't either."

"She talks like the mayor now," Peanuts grumbled.

That Detective Lamb, driving her own car, had gone in pursuit of what she recognized as a stolen vehicle and chased it through the streets of Fox River until running it to ground on a road paralleling the railroad tracks was more newsy than the poor devil who had somehow escaped before she could get out of her car and to him. The nearby area had been searched, to see if perhaps he had been thrown from the car.

"Stupid," was Peanuts's verdict. But on the radio Agnes was treated as a heroine. No wonder Peanuts did not want to be away from his car for long. Tuttle breathed a little prayer that Peanuts would not be tempted to duplicate Agnes's feat while he was in the passenger seat. Peanuts should have a Student Driver sign permanently affixed to the top of the car, as a warning to others.

It was later that day, on the six o'clock news that Tuttle heard the news that clarified his own day. Now he understood why he had been given the golden handshake by Burke, Wong, etc.

Stacey Wilson had dropped her appeal and fired her lawyers. She had confessed to the slaying of her husband and was resigned to serving the sentence that would be handed down.

THIRTY

WHEREVER TWO OR THREE are gathered together there is the possibility of disagreement, of maneuvering and resentment, of what on a larger scale is called politics. St. Hilary's parish was located in Fox River, Illinois, which had the look of one of those sleepy river towns that slide into view in *Life on the Mississippi* and show up as well in *Huckleberry Finn.* After the stress and pressure of the marriage tribunal, this parish had come to seem an untouched piece of Eden to Roger Dowling. He was the pastor and the only priest in the parish. It was his decision how things would go, but such decisions were risibly easy. Above all there had been an absence of dissent and resentment.

But Original Sin is everywhere and with time Roger Dowling realized that he was still in the Valley of Tears as well as the Fox River valley. Now he was confronted with the conflicting views of Marie Murkin and Edith Hospers about Elaine McCorkle.

"I already have help," Edith said. "Karen will be with me all year."

"And then what?" Marie asked, looking around as if seeking support from absent witnesses.

"She's also a volunteer," Edith added, addressing the pastor. "I should think Elaine's secretarial skills would be useful here in the house."

"You couldn't use her in that way?" Father Dowling asked. He had not fully appreciated before that Solomon had made enemies of both women in the case of the disputed child. This was altogether too much like the archdiocesan marriage tribunal. He must go counter to Marie or to Edith or perhaps both. The Solomonian solution that occurred to him was the employ Elaine part time in the rectory and part time at the parish center. Predictably both women frowned when he first broached this.

The meeting was being held at a table in the school gym, where the slap of cards, yelps of triumph and groans of failure, and the distinctive slide of the shuffleboard accompanied the discussion. It occurred to Roger Dowling that Marie had thought her point half won because the matter was being discussed in the center.

"You know our experience with help," Edith said.

Volunteers did come and go, the first fervor quickly vanishing before the daily task of being patient and attentive and cheerful with the senior parishioners, who sometimes brought the accumulated crankiness of decades into their retirement years. Their disabilities—failed hearing, dimming sight, and lack of agility—began to seem moral defects. They were a constant reminder of mortality.

"She can start by helping Marie," he decided.

Edith agreed, of course, and Marie could scarcely disagree.

"What do you expect me to have Elaine do?" Marie asked in controlled tones as they walked back to the rectory.

"Anything that will help relieve the burden you carry."

While Marie liked to remind him how herculean her burden was she had never done this as prelude to the suggestion that help for her be hired. Far from it. Father Dowling could see that her mind was already busy with the problem of how to use Elaine without using her.

"Given her inclinations, perhaps it would be best to have her do things in the church. She's forever making novenas and it was when I was fixing the May altar that this subject first came up."

"I don't need help in the sacristy." They had reached the back steps and the pastor stopped to make sure his words registerd with Marie.

"You'll have no one bothering you in your precious sacristy."

That had been an early victory over Marie, keeping her out of the sacristy. It had been her custom to lay out the vestments before Mass and to put them away afterward. She also had taken charge of the sacred vessels. It was when she showed up beside him when he was saying Mass, prepared to function as acolyte, that Father Dowling had acted. He much preferred to do all these things himself. Perhaps the cardinal was equivocal about altar girls, but Roger Dowling was not. And not only when female acolytes were as intrusive as Marie.

So it had come about that the only part of the church in which Marie had no responsibility was the sacristy. But that left the devotional altars, the vigil lights, and the magazine and book racks at the back of the church, where she made sure that *Crisis* always eclipsed the other monthly magazines. There was a rich arena of action for Elaine apart from the sacristy.

"Will you tell her or shall I?"

"Tell her what?"

"What have we been talking about?"

"How much have you said to her already?"

"I made no commitments," Marie said virtuously.

"Did you speak of salary?"

"I used the phrase 'starvation wage.'"

"I wonder what she earns downtown."

"Father, she doesn't expect anything like the salary she's been making."

"Well, I'll work it out with her. Do you have her number?"

"It's the same as Phil Keegan's," Marie said. The housekeeper was obviously thinking better of her campaign to get Elaine employed at St. Hilary's. "Maybe we should think about it some more."

"I have given it all the thought I mean to."

And in the study he called Phil and informed him that he intended to take Elaine on at the parish.

"You're crazy."

"That isn't what you said in your reference letter."

"If I told the truth, she'd never get a job."

"When is she finished there?"

"She goes on vacation next week."

"Is she there now?"

"I'll have to call her. But if you want my advice, you wouldn't rush into this."

Elaine, when he talked to her, said she wanted to start right away.

"I understand you go on vacation next week."

"I get paid for it, but I'm not going anywhere. I'd much rather start at St. Hilary's."

"Well, we're all looking forward to your being here. Marie and Edith and I discussed the matter. At the outset, you will be working with Marie, probably things in the church."

"Wonderful."

"We'll have to talk salary."

"Do you have a health plan?"

"Yes, we do."

"Father, that is all I really want. If you cover my health insurance, I will donate my services. My parents left me very comfortable."

"I can't take advantage of you like that, Elaine."

"Father, decide on a salary and I will claim that as a donation to St. Hilary's."

That her generosity might be offset by a tax advantage to her made it possible for Roger Dowling to accept.

STACEY WILSON'S withdrawal of her appeal brought only a shrug from Phil. "It was a fair trial, a fair verdict, a fair sentence."

"Amos Cadbury tells me her lawyers have genuinely new evidence that undermines the basis of the prosecution."

"Lawyers," Phil said with disgust. "A case is never over with those guys, so long as there's money or publicity to be had."

"Are you speaking of Amos?"

"Tell me why he got involved in this case."

"To represent a claimant to the Wilson fortune." No need to tell Phil that Amos had repented of that decision, in the sense that he had thought it far-fetched when Stacey's conviction was uncontested and regarded it as otiose in the light of discussion with her lawyers.

"Not a savory group," Amos said. "I might add in the confidentiality of our discussions that the Wilson estate is up against a kind of lawyer they have seldom dealt with."

"How do you mean?"

Whatever Amos meant he said it with great circumlocution. Father Dowling got the impression that Amos was saying that the firm that had come to Stacey's defense was often in the employ of those whose activities suggested traffic in drugs and women and the like.

"And gambling?"

Amos's white brows rose above the dark rims of his glasses and his mouth pursed beneath his white mustache. "I hope the police and prosecution will exhibit skepticism toward any new evidence produced by them."

But Phil informed him that the source of the firm's confidence that they could overturn the verdict was none other than Tuttle, Fox River's dubious contribution to the ranks of the legal profession. Amos too had known this.

"Tuttle," he murmured, his eyes lifting to the upper shelves of Father Dowling's bookcases.

"Not the most ethical member of the bar, Amos?"

"To be ethical or unethical invokes acknowledged standards. Tuttle, so far as I can discover, recognizes no standards. Perhaps he could be described as a-ethical. Or anethical. Alpha privative."

"Beyond good and evil?"

"Before good and evil."

Phil's attitude toward Tuttle was benevolent, tolerant. "He's a clown but he keeps Peanuts Pianone out of my hair."

Recent events had removed the Fox River police from further interest in the Stacey Wilson matter. She had confessed the crime and dropped the appeal. Her conviction stood. Tuttle's interview with Billy Wheaton, with all its ambiguity, sank from sight. Stacey's lawyers accepted their client's decision. Father Dowling could not believe that Phil had no curiosity left in this matter.

"Roger, I'm not paid to solve the riddle of the universe. I've got a deskful of things I don't understand."

It seemed time to make another visit to Joliet. As Father Dowling pulled away from the rectory, the little minibus with Karen at the wheel and a young man beside her turned into the driveway.

THIRTY-ONE

"WALTER NICKLES," Keegan repeated, looking up at Cy Horvath. The lieutenant's face was as inscrutable to Keegan as a map of the Eastern European country from which Horvath's people had come.

"We called it a suicide."

"Jolson called it a suicide," Keegan corrected. They were guided by the judgment of the medical examiner and the coroner's verdict.

"You ever met Pippin?"

"Scottie?" Keegan did not intend the mention of the Pippin who played for the Chicago Bulls as a joke but when Cy actually laughed Keegan took credit.

"Monique Pippin. No reason why you should. She started to work for Jolson just to fill in time, before going to Mayo's for a residency, then got hooked on forensic medicine."

"Yeah?"

Keegan had just located the name Walter Nickles. The poor devil who had been found dead in his bathtub, allegedly despondent over an unhappy romance. With Elaine McCorkle! Why would he have difficulty remembering that?

"Pippin thinks it's impossible that he killed himself."

"What does Jolson think?"

"That she's nuts."

Phil tried not to sigh audibly in relief. It was the trait of the novice, seeking problems where no problems were. Young detectives often doubted that any death was accidental and begged to be allowed to continue an investigation. There were too many open-and-shut murders to permit that.

"Jolson's a man of experience."

"Right. And the lungs were full of water, no sign of violence, no bruises, contusions or broken bones."

"But Monica Pippin suspects foul play nonetheless?"

"Monique. Here's why."

Keegan stared down at the form Cy had put before him. If he picked it up and read it, he would be, if only tentatively, agreeing that some greenhorn in Jolson's operation knew more than the boss. He kept his hands on the arms of his chair, but his eyes scanned the form as if they had a mind of their own.

"What's her story?"

"The reason it went so smoothly, as if he did it himself, was that he was full of tranquilizer." Cy's meaty index finger pointed to an entry on the form.

Keegan looked up in disappointment. "Cy, the man probably gobbled up the pills so he could go through with it."

"There were no tranquilizers in the apartment."

"He ate them all."

"The container too?"

Keegan kept his patience. It was a slow time, that was part of the problem. Their minds had little to work on except a case already settled and now that Stacey Wilson had withdrawn her appeal the Marvin Wilson murder was definitely history. Besides, Cy was his best man. He had trained him himself. That is why he kept the sarcasm out of his voice when he suggested the tranquilizers could have been taken somewhere outside the apartment, and that Nickles could have disposed of the container. His hands lifted from the arms of his chair, opened as if to let in a world of possible explanations. Cy nodded through it all, in total agreement.

"So what are you telling me?"

"Pippin checked out Nickles's vehicle. No tranquilizers or container there. But she ran a check on a fast-food malted cup that was in the car. It was loaded with tranquilizers.

Again Keegan stifled his sarcasm. Cy should know as well as he that this meant nothing. Even as Cy spoke, Keegan imagined Nickles loading up the malted, chucking the tranquilizer container out the window of his car, going home and, before going up to do the fateful deed, downing the loaded drink. Dutch courage, as Phil's father used to call booze.

"Why don't you check it out, Cy."

"It's probably nothing."

"Even so."

If there was anything there, Cy would find it, but Keegan had no illusions on that score. As soon as something else happened, as God knows it surely would, he would put Cy on it. Meantime, it was just as well to have him working on something, however remote. He himself was whiling away this crime lull in Fox River by harassing Tuttle.

Two hours later Tuttle shuffled into Keegan's office and hesitated next to the chair, waiting to be asked to sit. Keegan let him stand.

"Keep your hat on, Tuttle."

Tuttle took off his hat.

"Don't sit down."

Tuttle sat. "How can I help you, Captain Keegan?"

"I'd like you to turn over all the evidence you have in criminal cases."

Tuttle put his hat back on and chuckled. His chuckle died when Keegan read him the riot act about selling taped interviews to Stacey Wilson's lawyers.

"Your quarrel is with her counsel, not with me, Captain. In turning those tapes over to Mrs. Wilson's lawyers, I was of course making them available to the criminal justice system. As an officer of the court I could do no less. Needless to say, evidence is equally accessible to prosecution and defense, at the proper time. I resent the implication of your remark, Captain."

"Implication, hell. I'm accusing you of obstructing justice, withholding evidence, misusing public property."

"Public property?"

"I know you use Pianone as your personal chauffeur, Tuttle. The car he drives belongs to the city."

"And I am a grateful citizen, Captain. Officer Pianone should be decorated for volunteering to assist me in the opportunity to provide the court more evidence in the—"

"Shut up, Tuttle. I'll leave it in the hands of the prosecutor."

"Thank God. Fellow lawyers will understand."

Keegan glowered at him. Of course Tuttle was right. Tuttle had been up before committees of the local bar half a dozen times but the most he had received was a slap on the wrist. No wonder. His examiners were little better than he was. The only exception was Amos Cadbury. What did Amos Cadbury make of this sudden move on the part of Stacey Wilson's lawyers? After Tuttle left, Keegan decided to find out.

Getting through to the lawyer was the kind of challenge Keegan liked.

"Who should I say is calling?"

"It's confidential."

"I cannot put an anonymous call through to Mr. Cadbury."

"Just tell him it's the police."

"The Chicago police?"

Miss Cleary was something. "No Fox River."

"To whom am I speaking?"

"Is this the office of Amos Cadbury?"

"I must know who you are before I divulge my identity."

"Why don't you get an unlisted number if you don't want to answer inquiries?"

"One moment, please." In a moment she spoke again. "Captain Keegan, I'll put you through to Mr. Cadbury."

"How the hell did you know?" Keegan demanded.

"Know what, Captain?" came the patrician voice of Amos Cadbury. "Did you think I wouldn't recognize your voice?"

"If your secretary ever wants to make a lateral move in her career, I'd like to hire her as press liaison for the Fox River police."

"Is that the position Miss McCorkle held?"

Was it public knowledge that Elaine had left? Doubtless Amos's informant was Roger Dowling. It seemed an odd bit of information to pass on to the lawyer. Could Mr. Cadbury find time to talk with Captain Keegan? Of course. They could have drinks at the Cliffdwellers at five. Keegan said that he'd be there.

Private clubs grated on Keegan, not least because they were seldom luxurious. The bar of the Cliffwellers couldn't compete with any reasonably popular hotel lounge. The wooden tables were scarred, the chairs uncomfortable, but there was no nonsense about smoking and he lit up his cigar while Cadbury watched with envy.

"Mr. Cadbury, what do you conclude from the switch on the part of Stacey Wilson's lawyers?"

"Withdrawing the appeal?"

"Yes."

"That she is innocent."

"Innocent?"

"Does a guilty killer ever give up, admit what he or she has done, and ask to be punished?"

"I'll grant you it's rare. But why would she give up?"

"She's frightened."

Keegan thought about it. His scotch and water came. Cadbury was drinking sweet vermouth but he seemed to wish he was having scotch and water too.

"Mr. Cadbury, you know what it's like in prison. Any prison. Some are worse than others but they're all bad. She's seen enough of them to know that. She should be doing everything she can to get out of there. She'd have to be scared to death."

"That is my guess."

Amos Cadbury admitted that he was disappointed that his client was now back in the picture. Stacey's decision made it definitive that she could inherit none of her late husband's wealth.

"That means the eagles will gather. My client prominent among them. Have you ever speculated on the amount of money that comes to people without labor or merit on their part? The lottery aside, of course. That money is collected for random allocation. But earned wealth, estates, copyrights, royalties, things that men and women accumulate by the sweat of their brows and which turn out to be less mortal than their makers. The surviving wealth must be claimed by someone. Governments get their share, of course, but there is a vast army of beneficiaries of the work of their forebears or relatives, however remote. Their main exertion is to hire a lawyer to go get it."

"Don't expect me to be critical of the legal profession, Mr. Cadbury."

The older man put down his glass carefully before acknowledging that he grasped Keegan's muffled sarcasm.

"As we are unequivocal admirers of the constabulary, Captain."

Amos Cadbury thought that Stacey Jones Wilson's long sojourn in Las Vegas had brought her into touch with the mob. It was the mob who had come to her rescue when she was accused of her husband's death. Had she been the agent of the mob in marrying Marvin, the way to his wealth? Obviously something had gone wrong. Say she was out of town, as she said. Then someone else killed Marvin Wilson. A professional job? Nothing told for or against it. But if Stacey lost, so did the mob if they were in it and the money was going to go to Virginia Wilson's convent and Amos Cadbury's client.

"Will the police now simply drop out of the picture, Captain?"

"We already have."

"And that is why you called me? Why we have met here?"

"Call it personal curiosity."

"May I tell you what I wish that personal curiosity might lead to? Good. I presume you could call on police in Nevada for help. It could be very interesting to know more of Stacey Wilson's life in the Las Vegas casinos. Wouldn't it be interesting if it were learned that she was in Las Vegas when she supposedly was dispatching her husband to a better world?"

"Remind me not to become your client."

"Oh, my client wants only what is rightfully his."

And there they left it. But Keegan liked the idea. It was a way to get Cy off the Nickles suicide and back onto something important.

THIRTY-TWO

IF STACEY HAD NOT ALREADY decided to keep from Tyrone the information on how to make use of the numbers she had given him, the news from Las Vegas would have done it. Almost from the time she had told Tyrone of the card in her purse, she regretted it. The Swiss account was her private insurance, the certainty that she would come out of her marriage to Marvin with something. There was $135,000 in the account. Not a fortune, but hers, a tribute in part to Marvin's generosity to her, particularly at first. She distracted Tyrone from the account by telling him of the insurance. The insurance policy had been a mistake, Ron's idea.

Had she ever thought it was just an innocent suggestion? When she talked with Tyrone after returning from Vegas, she thought he was conning her, taking credit for something Ron had arranged.

"Thanks for letting me get out of town first anyway."

Tyrone lifted his brows, rolled out his lower lip, and shrugged. An admission? What else was she to think? It put her on the spot when to her vast surprise she was accused of killing Marvin.

She couldn't say she was in Vegas with Ron, she couldn't say anything that would direct attention to Vegas. The law firm from Chicago was affiliated with firms she had become aware of in Nevada and she had felt in good hands. She was stuck with the story about being at the farm but the only thing the prosecution had was some old rummy's story about seeing her in the boat. Stacey had thought the truth would be enough. She hadn't been in the boat and that was that. But the unreliable eyewitness was believed. It took a while but finally an effective counter to that testimony had been found. Stacey figured to be outside and rich within weeks.

And then came the shattering news that changed everything.

Ron dead. Found floating in his swimming pool, face down, an ugly wound on the back of his head. Ron never swam. That pool had been for his whining wife and rotten kids. The accident was attributed to the amount of tranquilizer in his blood. That Ron took tranquilizers was news to Stacey.

At first her suspicions seemed fantastic, but eventually they became cold certainty. Had Tyrone thought that Ron would defy everything, his associates, his family, the tradition, and come forward to establish her alibi and win her freedom? Fat chance.

Hasser, the lawyer, didn't know what to say when she told him to drop the appeal. As a lawyer he knew that was legal suicide, but he couldn't keep a flicker of relief from his eyes either. They would rather have her in prison than running around free because who knew what she would do or say eventually?

What she refused to do was walk out the gate and become a wealthy woman, because the first knock at the door would be the one who killed Ron. The killer had taken on a face. Tyrone's.

Her son was a stranger. She didn't know him. He didn't know her. She didn't give a damn about genetic codes and all the rest of it. There was more than biology involved. He was as much the product of Mrs. Plaisance and all the institutions he had spent time in as he was of her womb.

It had to have been Tyrone in the boat with Marvin. Marvin could handle a boat that length alone in normal weather but going out on a day like that he would have accepted an offer to crew even from a kid he'd once thought was a gigolo. A cap pulled down tight on Tyrone's head might have acted as a disguise. Tyrone had as much as told her he'd done it, but he would have picked up the art of bullshit. Easy to claim credit for something that couldn't be proved one way or the other. But she believed it now.

He had gotten rid of her husband, he had gotten rid of her lover, and no doubt he would get rid of her too when he figured out some way to inherit it all.

Stacey bit her lip thinking of the impulse that had led her to tell him of the card in her purse. The numbers were the numbers of the Swiss account, the legend was the name of the bank. She had given him everything but instructions on how to get into that account. At the time she had thought it a genuinely maternal desire, to provide for her poor abandoned son. The little nest egg she had set aside for herself would be his; even if her conviction was not overturned, he would get it.

Thank God she had not explained the whole procedure of Swiss banking.

God? In her cell, Stacey kept her TV turned to a religious cable channel but with the sound off. Preaching, praying, singing, healing—she watched it all with a vague distaste.

"It's a free country," Father Dowling said when she asked him about it.

"Most of it looks about as religious as the chapel I married Marvin in."

"Do you believe in God?"

No one had ever asked her that before. It was not a question she wanted to answer. Was it the priest's duty to ask? Stacey engaged a lot in what she sometimes thought of as praying, but it was like talking to herself. Only it couldn't be herself, or if it was she was holding herself to account and she hadn't invented the standards of appraisal.

"I don't know."

He didn't press it. "How old is your son?"

"Son? I don't have a son."

THIRTY-THREE

THERE ARE MANY REASONS why a parent might repudiate a child, and vice versa, but Father Dowling was startled by Stacey's answer. The cigarettes she smoked came in maroon boxes and were concealed beneath flaps of golden paper. Getting one out gave her a chance to compose herself. He had no doubt that she was lying but was certain that she would continue to lie if he pressed her. He let it go.

Walking back to the prison chaplain's office, he considered the other possibilities. Either Elaine had lied to him about the odd claim that Tyrone Pajakowski had made in order to persuade her to show him the evidence in the Stacey Wilson case, which he considered highly unlikely, or Stacey did not know she had a son. Would the young man show such interest in his mother's trial and not visit her himself?

"It's her brother," the chaplain said, after making a call.

Which might have settled that perhaps if he had not signed the register as Tyrone Pajakowski.

"Pajakowski," Cy Horvath said when Roger Dowling asked him what Stacey's married name had been.

Her visitor could have been a brother-in-law, perhaps, but certainly not a brother. In any case, it was difficult to know what to make of it. If the man had lied to Elaine, calling himself Stacey Wilson's son, that was hardly a significant addition to the deception he had already practiced.

Twice Dowling had listened to Elaine pour out her heart on the topic of what a silly fool she had been with Tyrone.

"It was vain for me to think he was interested in me. Look at me."

Not the kind of remark to which he could respond, of course. He busied himself knocking ashes from his pipe.

"Besides he is much younger."

"How old would you say he is?"

"Five years younger than I am."

Roger Dowling had the impression she had done a little subtracting before coming up with that figure. He listened to Elaine as a pastoral duty, feeling more pity than sympathy for her. Whatever was to be said about her attractions, he was emphatically no judge of that, having been astonished more than once by the couples he met. Ugly men attracted beautiful women just as women apparently unblessed with beauty often drew handsome men. If there were logic in such matters, it seemed certain that Elaine had been destined for Walter Nickles. But she had left him for Tyrone, and Walter, finding abandonment unbearable, drowned himself in his tub.

Or such at least had been received opinion until a minority view formed in the medical examiner's office. Phil mentioned it as an annoyance, the zeal of a junior pathologist seizing upon the fact that the body had been full of tranquilizers.

"Wouldn't that have been noticed immediately, I mean in the autopsy?"

"It was."

"Just what does full of tranquilizers mean?"

"Enough to make drowning in a tub seem less stupid."

"Enough to kill him?"

"He died by drowning."

"There's no quarrel about that?"

Jolson and his assistant were as one in concluding that Walter Nickles had died of drowning. It was the question of suicide that Monique Pippin thought was called into question by the presence of the tranquilizers.

"So it's not a medical difference?"

Phil brightened. "Exactly. She wants to play detective."

But the more Phil said of young Dr. Pippin's views the more intriguing they seemed to the pastor of St. Hilary's. No need to antagonize his old friend by saying so, of course. Particularly when he learned a good deal more by being another old codger who would appreciate Phil Keegan's impatience with the young.

"Was Walter an edgy man?" he asked Elaine when her lamentation had turned from her folly with Tyrone to her ingratitude toward Walter.

"I don't understand."

"Nervous. Jumpy."

She made a little noise with her lips. "He was calm and confident. He looked frail but if he had looked like his voice and the way he acted, well..."

"Did he take tranquilizers?"

"Walter? He was already the way people take tranquilizers to become."

"He couldn't have kept it a secret from you?"

In response she told him of the way in which Walter would tell her everything about himself, whether she wanted to hear or not. It was his way of strengthening the bond between them—his secrets were hers, there was no barrier between them.

"I told him nothing. Almost nothing. When I met Tyrone I didn't tell Walter. He couldn't have deceived me if he tried. He did find out, though, and actually threatened Tyrone."

Even now, she told of it from Tyrone's point of view, his masterful handling of the situation. Poor Walter came through as the inept wimp who compounded his defeat by making it known to a stranger.

"Was Tyrone jealous of Walter?"

Her laugh sounded like a sob. She shook her head and tears came from her squeezed-shut eyes.

"How did he take it when Walter died?"

But she seemed to think questions about what Tyrone thought of Walter meant Father Dowling had not yet understood what a fool she'd been.

"Father, he was just using me. He wanted to get into the Black Museum. That's all. Captain Keegan saw that immediately; so did Lieutenant Horvath. Afterward I was of no further use to him."

She had tried, of course, even claiming that it was she who had stolen the missing car found near Tyrone's motel unit. Cy had arrested Tyrone, who might have landed back in prison for violating parole if the girl who had been in the unit with him when Elaine arrived had not driven off in the stolen car while Cy was in the unit. He came out with Tyrone, with Elaine protesting that she was the one who had stolen the car. She could not point it out when asked to, however; the car was gone. Three hours later the car was pursued by Agnes Lamb and crashed, but was found empty. A search for any proof Tyrone had been in the car, let alone driven it, proved fruitless. After a week in the Fox River jail, Tyrone Pajakowski was once more free as the breeze.

"But you did see him after showing him that evidence?"

"Yes, but I knew then it was all a pretense. He was letting me down easy. There were other women..." She stopped in deference to the surroundings, but Roger had heard it all from Horvath and Keegan. If Elaine wanted someone to agree with her that she was a fool to think Tyrone had been attracted by her womanly charms, she had Phil Keegan's vote.

"But the visit to the Black Museum turned out to be pointless."

"It was bound to be, Father. He expected to find proof that she was his mother. He seemed to think she carried his birth certificate around in her purse." Elaine shook her head, and the tears began again.

"And he didn't find it?"

She seemed not to understand.

"There wasn't anything in the evidence that proved he was the son of Stacey Wilson, was there?"

"He didn't find his birth certificate, no."

For Elaine that awful evening had culminated when Captain Keegan and Lieutenant Horvath suddenly appeared in the tunnel.

"I just blurted out that he was the son of Stacey Wilson, as if that explained everything."

"Tell me what you did find among the evidence."

"The only thing he wanted to see was her purse. I opened that and he looked into it and that was that."

"Didn't you take anything out?"

"Well, yes. I mean, there were just the usual things."

Roger Dowling considered that scene, the duped unattractive older woman showing the young man the contents of a drawer containing evidence used in the trial of a woman he claimed was his mother. Would Tyrone have just stood there patiently while Elaine looked through the purse?

"He could see the things as well as I could."

"But he didn't take anything?"

She rubbed her eyes and inhaled, then shook her head. "What he wanted wasn't there, Father."

She still did not see that this left his claim to be the son of Stacey Wilson only that. "Did he have any other proof?"

"Father, he didn't doubt it. I mean, I knew who my parents were but I might still want proof of it."

Certificates of birth and baptism and the like were seldom used to remove skeptical doubts, she was right about that. They simply certified what was already known.

"Then what was the point?"

"He had to know. Don't you see how different it must have been for him. It was like someone who had been adopted who wanted to find out his true parents."

It made no sense to Roger Dowling, but then not much of Elaine's story did. Working at St. Hilary's had removed Elaine from harm's way. As far as Father Dowling knew, she had not seen Tyrone since coming to work at the parish. Of course she continued to live at home and he had no idea what she did then, but Marie Murkin dismissed his question with a wave of her hand.

"You'll never understand women, Father Dowling."

"I couldn't agree more."

"Oh, it isn't just because you're a priest. You're a man."

Marie smiled smugly, secure in the conviction that the mysteries of the female heart were closed to the prying curiosity of men. Her own curiosity had been satisfied in the case of Tyrone, it seemed. She hadn't a doubt in the world that he was a closed chapter in the life of Elaine. Perhaps. But when Father Dowling asked if she had a photograph of the young man, she produced one from her wallet.

Looking into the sly wise face, at the smile that seemed a decoy, the priest saw immediately the quintessential deceiver. Would he have thought that if he didn't know Elaine's story?

"Stacey Wilson's not his mother, Elaine."

She took back the picture as if to protect Tyrone from his skepticism.

"I asked her, Elaine. She says she has no son."

"You talked with her?"

"Yes. I visited her in prison." It seemed a biblical remark, and he added hastily, lest he seem to be claiming too much. "A friend of mine is chaplain there."

But Elaine was considering what he said. Finally she murmured, "Of course that's what she would say."

"Why?"

Roger Dowling thought he was going to get another statement on the mysteries of a woman's heart. But what Elaine meant was that a mother would not want to involve a child in her troubles.

"No parent would."

And Roger Dowling thought of Earl Hospers who would not let Edith bring any of their kids along on her visits to Joliet.

THIRTY-FOUR

IN GRADE SCHOOL Elaine had been told of earlier times when penitents were assigned difficult deeds to make up for their sins, a pilgrimage to a far-off shrine, public penance befitting a public sinner, anything but the few Our Fathers and Hail Marys that had become standard long before Elaine was prepared for her first confession. She had always dreaded going to confession no matter how much she told herself that the priest was there doing what Christ had told him to do. Whose sins you shall forgive, they are forgiven. She tried to imagine Our Lord himself on the other side of the grille, listening patiently to her recital of sins. But the confessional was claustrophobic and hot, and no matter how hard she tried to ignore the unintelligible whisper of another penitent on the opposite side of the priest she was aware of it because when it stopped the grille would open and she would confess. But talking to Father Dowling in his rectory study was almost enjoyable.

No matter how foolish she might feel telling him about Tyrone she never had the sense that the pastor thought she was foolish. Without diminishing her troubles, he convinced her that everyone had a similar story to tell.

"There's nothing more than foolishness to confess?" he asked.

She looked unseeingly at the backs of books on the shelf behind him. "I would have done anything for him."

"Only thoughts?"

She nodded. Except that wasn't her fault, or rather the opposite. When she got rid of that girl and was helping Tyrone clean up the motel unit she was in a mood to do anything he asked. She stood beside the bed and looked boldly at him but it seemed not to enter his mind that she might want to do with him on that bed what that scrawny little girl had done. Sinful as those thoughts had been, they had been only thoughts.

"I'll give you absolution."

"Like confession?"

He unrolled a little stole and put it over his shoulders. When he began to pray, she knelt on the floor of the study and for the first time realized that what she had done was sinful, not just foolish. What a relief it was to receive absolution and put it all behind her.

Except the shaming memories, of course. Telling Father Dowling had been easy; avoiding Marie Murkin's nosiness was something else.

"Just ignore her," Edith Hospers said. "That's what I do."

"She acts as if she has a right to know everything."

In Edith, she had a real ally. Elaine almost regretted stirring up Edith's anger at the housekeeper. Clearly there was no love lost between those two. It took away from her sense that St. Hilary's was a little island of peace in a dog-eat-dog world.

It was when she was sitting in Edith's office that she looked out and saw Tyrone in the playground, talking with some of the old people. She ended the conversation abruptly and fled from the school, going out the front door and circling around to the church where she went up into the choir loft and sat in a huddle and trembled at the realization that she had wanted to run out there and throw herself in Tyrone's arms.

In her wallet, next to the picture of Tyrone, was the little calling card he had taken from his mother's purse in the Black Museum. He had given it to her and she had told him she would return it to the purse, but she never had. For one thing, she never intended to go again into the Black Museum. For another, the card was a remembrance of Tyrone.

Why had she run? Confessing to Father Dowling had been the turning over of a new page. It had meant that her folly about Tyrone was over. But she did not want it over, she didn't care how foolish it was. Did she want to stay at St. Hilary's and become like Marie

Murkin or even Edith Hospers? She sat up and looked over the railing toward the sanctuary and the flickering red lamp over the tabernacle.

"Help me," she whispered.

But even as she said it, she rose, clattered down the steps and ran back to the school.

There was no sign of Tyrone on the playground and when she went into the auditorium there were only old people playing cards, no Tyrone, no Karen, no Edith.

"Can I help you, dear?" an old woman said.

"Have you seen Karen?" It would be easier to ask the girl than Edith.

"She's gone off in the bus." the woman said.

"With her boyfriend," said her partner, not looking up from her cards.

Boyfriend? What did he look like? A babble of voices but the image of Tyrone emerged from the descriptions. Elaine thought of that young snip he had had with him in the motel. Had Karen taken that girl's place? Elaine in her agitation was prepared to believe anything. She imagined Tyrone and Karen tumbling on the motel bed. She turned and fled.

THIRTY-FIVE

THE FIRST TIME Karen mentioned Elaine, Tyrone hadn't made the connection. Elaine worked in the courthouse; it couldn't be the same woman who worked at St. Hilary's. The second time, it was clear that Elaine was new at the parish and he asked about it. Not that it was any big deal. He didn't want to run into her when he went out to see Karen, but if he did, so what? Elaine was a fat and unattractive older woman who represented a so-far failed effort to get at the money Stacey had squirreled away.

"I'll tell you later," Stacey said, when she first mentioned it. "Don't be so damned nosey."

Bullshit? Maybe. It was hard to tell. She wasn't easy to get any kind of information out of. He should have suspected then that there had been someone in Vegas, but when they talked about the insurance policy, Stacey had given no indication. Tyrone didn't like the idea of the insurance policy but she answered that by saying she was also putting away cash against a rainy day. It had sounded like a safe deposit box.

Then Wilson's body was found and Tyrone almost laughed out loud when Stacey told him in hushed tones that she thought it was murder.

"Yeah?"

This was before the rummy told his story. But she wasn't thinking of Tyrone, she was thinking of Vegas. Her problem was she didn't know if it was the guy or his friends.

"Or enemies?"

That got to her. It explained why she went through the trial without a murmur and now seemed to think she was safer in Joliet than she would be outside. She had a lot to learn about prison if she believed that.

It was Karen who made him realize that he had not put in all that time with fatso Elaine for nothing. She was a college girl, Karen, smart, she even knew foreign languages. Just for fun, to test her, he asked her what *Caisse* meant.

"Bank? Something to do with a bank?" Her nose moved in a rabbity way as she thought. Tyrone fished out the slip on which he had written down what had been on the card in Stacey's purse.

"A foreign account? My, my, I had no idea."

"Foreign. Is that the closest you can come?"

"Switzerland?"

Three oranges plunked into place in the slot machine of his mind. "Wrong," he said, and changed the subject.

Doing Wilson and the guy in Vegas had not been pointless after all. Walter had been for himself. He just didn't like to be told what he could or could not do, especially by a jerk like Walter. Imagine fighting over Elaine. Well, Walter had taken a final bath. Tyrone loaded up a malted with Valium when he and Walter got together. Later he took Walter back to his place, ran a tub of water, stripped him down to his shorts, and dumped him into the tub. There hadn't even been much of a struggle.

Tyrone hadn't liked the thought that he had devoted all that time and effort to nothing. And Stacey got coy.

"What cash?"

"That you were stashing away."

She pretended to try to remember, then shook her head slowly. "Where did you get an idea like that?"

"Something you said."

Just like that, she was mad as hell. "Why did you have to look me up? If I hadn't taken out that insurance policy, it wouldn't have happened, I wouldn't be here."

"Yeah?"

"Yeah. And now it won't do either of us any good."

After her appeal was withdrawn, she didn't want to see him, she didn't want to talk. She was scared. Tyrone had seen that kind of fear before. She would be better off on the run than as a sitting duck at Joliet. She jumped to her feet when he told her that, and the visit was over.

But she had come through finally, telling him about the purse, and that had led to all the business with Elaine, getting at the evidence, snatching the card. Thinking of that card back in the purse made him uneasy. Why the hell had he told Elaine to put it back? What if they had gone over that evidence again, wondering what he had been looking for, and found the card? Of course they'd find the card. He had wanted it back because he was afraid someone would miss it. Eventually someone would figure out what it meant. What if he got all the way to Switzerland and found out the account had been cleaned out already?

"TYRONE? This is Elaine."

Ten in the morning, and he had been awakened by the phone.

"Tyrone?"

"Yeah, how are you?"

"I want to see you."

"Good, fine. I'm just about to take a trip, but when I get back..."

"I want to give you something. Remember the card you took from your mother's purse?"

Tyrone sat up in bed, fully awake now. "What are you talking about?"

"I still have it. I didn't put it back. I thought you might want it."

Her tone was wistful, wheedling, the whine of the loser, but it was like music in his ears.

"You still have it?"

"I kept thinking you should have something, you know?"

He swung his feet to the floor and sat on the edge of the bed. "How'd you like a Chinese lunch?"

"I've found a place that might be better than the Great Wall."

The address she gave was out by St. Hilary's. He didn't let on that he knew she wasn't working downtown anymore.

"I'll be there."

After he hung up, he continued to sit on the edge of his bed. He wanted to do this right. He would get the card and then do Elaine. He wanted to leave Fox River clean, with no one able to figure out where he had gone. Karen didn't count. She thought he was someone named Gordon. Karen. Then he had it. Of course. Elaine could take her last ride in St. Hilary's minibus.

THIRTY-SIX

IF MARIE MURKIN had suggested he visit Tyrone Pajakowski he would have found a dozen reasons to say no. Even going on his own, certainly without telling Marie, Father Dowling was still debating with himself when he pulled into the parking lot of the motel. Once it had been part of a national chain, but that had been years ago. Now the motel had passed into private hands. Gutters hung uncertainly from eaves, plastic and plaster was faded and chipped, half the units lacked identifying numerals. The pool area was surrounded by a fence. It should have been empty, full of debris, cracked and crumbling. Surprisingly, it was brim full of sparkling blue water. The woman in the office turned when he entered and her expression became one of almost terror.

"I'm Father Dowling, pastor of St. Hilary's."

Her mouth was slack, her eyes wide, she seemed to be translating his words into a more intelligible idiom.

"You want a room?" Incredulity in her tone.

"I believe Tyrone Pajakowski is staying here."

Relief swept over her face and she grinned. "You here to see him?"

"Is he in?"

"I don't know."

"Could you call his unit?"

"This phone don't work. He's in seven."

That seemed to be it. He feared if he stayed there she would be calling for others to come see the priest. As he walked toward unit 7, Roger Dowling remembered seminary days when he had gone through the phase of imagining himself a missionary. Wearing a white cassock and pith helmet, he would be a stranger in a strange land, a mysterious and exotic figure. But that is what he was now in Fox River in the Easy Times Inn. The country had entered a post-Christian phase and he might have come from outer space.

A cleaning cart was parked between units 7 and 8 and the door of 7 was open. He tapped on the door, but the roar of the television made his knock inaudible. A shapeless black woman in a faded pink uniform stood by the bed, her weight on one foot, a hand on her hip, staring at the television. He tapped her shoulder and she turned. If the woman in the office had been frightened by the sight of a priest the cleaning lady actually leapt, springing away from him, going into a crouch as if she considered herself in danger.

"I ain't done yet!" she screamed over the sound of the television.

Her fright seemed to give him *droit de cité*. He nodded and looked around the room. The bed was stripped but not yet made. Behind the door was a rack where a limited wardrobe hung. Two pairs of tennis shoes seemed an index of affluence. The cleaning lady had circled behind the table over which a lamp hung from a looped chain. She seemed to think he was the occupant returned too soon. The door of the bathroom was open and the light on. His eye was caught by the array of glass and plastic bottles. One did not need a degree in pharmacy to see that Tyrone Pajakowski was a devotee of preventive medicine, of sleeping pills and pep pills, vitamins of all sorts in jumbo-size jars. Nonprescription drugs predominated but there were prescription drugs as well. The label on the almost-empty king-size Valium bottle was from Stillwater, a correctional institution in Minnesota. It required an inner struggle not to take that bottle with him when he left.

When he stepped outside, the television in the unit was turned off and the sudden silence made him turn. The cleaning lady, still in a crouch, looked warily after him. He raised his hand in farewell and she scratched a sign of the cross over her pink bosom.

His impulse was to get in touch with Monique Pippin but that could wait. Thank God Elaine had come to work at St. Hilary's where she was out of harm's way. This feeling passed quickly. Elaine was still obsessed with Tyrone. Moreover, Father Dowling could not believe Elaine could have been unaware of Tyrone's devotion to soft drugs. But what did it mean? It made no sense to think that Tyrone had wanted to rid himself of a rival for Elaine's affection. Elaine might have wanted to rid herself of her pesky admirer, but what motive would Elaine have to load Walter up with tranquilizers and drown him in a bathtub? One thing however was sure: Tyrone had the means.

"Have you seen Elaine?" he asked Marie Murkin after returning from the motel, before going over to say the noon mass.

"She's around."

She was not in evidence in the church and, after mass, he stopped by the school.

"She went someplace for lunch, Father, bad news. The minibus is missing."

"Missing?"

"Gone, we can't find it. Karen was going to take a group downtown to see the exhibit at the Rush Museum and found the minibus was gone."

"Could Elaine have taken it?"

"Oh, she wouldn't have done that."

"Have you reported it?"

"Do you think I should?"

"I'll do it."

Edith walked with him to the door where she whispered, "Elaine didn't take it. Have you met Gordon?"

"Who's Gordon?"

"He's been here a couple of times, to see Karen."

"An old man?"

"No, no. Young. The funny thing is, he came for Elaine."

He realized that Edith was keeping this from Karen. "How old is Gordon?"

"Younger than Elaine."

"Describe him."

It was a preoccupied pastor who ate the lunch Marie Murkin put before him. When he had finished, he would have had trouble remembering what he had eaten.

"Did you find Elaine?"

"Is she back?"

"Back?"

He went to his study and lit a pipe, but he could not concentrate on the book he opened. Dante is not to be read when distracted. He closed the book, stood and then went forcefully down the hall and out the front door. A minute later, he was again on his way to the Easy Times Inn.

The minibus was parked by unit 7. Father Dowling approached the door and was about to knock when sounds from the pool distracted him, voices, a man's, the giggle of a woman. He turned. Elaine, reclining in a beach chair, followed the chatter of the young man who leaned toward her. Tyrone. More laughter and then he handed her a glass. They toasted and Tyrone solicitously watched her drink.

Roger Dowling turned away and tried the door of unit 7. It opened. He stepped inside, left the door ajar, and crossed to the bathroom. The plastic bottle of Valium from Stillwater lay on its side in the medicine cabinet, all but empty.

There was a telephone beside the bed and Roger Dowling hesitated to use it. He should call Phil, get help, but in the meantime a tranquilized Elaine might drown in the motel pool.

He picked up the phone and his decision seemed made for him when he heard the sound of voices on the line. It was in use. And then he recognized the voice of the woman in the motel office. Had she lied to him about the phones earlier?

"Excuse me," Roger Dowling barked, imitating Phil Keegan. "This is an official call. Go immediately to the pool and ask that young man with the girl to come to the phone."

"Who is this?"

"I said immediately!"

"You mean Tyrone?"

"Go!" Father Dowling roared.

Silence and then the sound of the instrument being put down. There was still the rasp of breathing on the line. The cord of the phone was not long enough to permit him to go to the door and look out. He dropped the phone on the bed and went to the door and looked toward the pool. Tyrone frowned up at the woman who was gesturing toward the office. Would he go to the phone? What seemed a full minute passed. Roger Dowling stared at the tableau by the motel pool. The woman from the office held her expectant pose, Elaine smiled woozily at the world, Tyrone looked at the woman, at the office, then slowly looked about him.

Suddenly he smiled, shrugged, and hopped to his feet. His swimming trunks were a study in indecency. He put his arm about the round shoulders of the woman and went with her to the office.

Roger Dowling stepped outside and went to the minibus. The keys were in the ignition. He got quickly behind the wheel, started the motor and backed up. A moment later, he had shifted into drive and was headed at increasing speed toward the office of the motel.

When the vehicle bumped over the concrete edge of the patio he was thrown off balance and before he could right himself and brake the vehicle he had crashed into the office doorway, effectively imprisoning Tyrone.

He hopped out of the minibus and went through the pool enclosure to Elaine, took the towel that was draped over the chair in which Tyrone had sat and covered her with it. She smiled up at him.

"Father Dowling," she said dreamily. "What brings you here?"

The approaching wail of a siren, summoned by the terrified motel clerk, might have been an answer to her question. A minute later, a Fox River squad car squealed into the motel entrance and approached between the units, lights flashing, its siren shrill. The car's doors opened like wings and two officers emerged, guns drawn, and advanced on the minibus.

"The window," Father Dowling shouted. "The side window."

Tyrone was half in, half out, when the police reached him. They pulled him outside. He was at a disadvantage in his ridiculous bikini, but he quickly recovered his aplomb.

"What's this all about, officers?"

But the lilt went out of his voice when he saw Father Dowling approach.

"A stolen vehicle," the priest said. "To start at the end."

"Hey, Father, I borrowed it. Karen said I could use it."

"Call Captain Keegan," Roger Dowling advised the officers. "And Lieutenant Horvath."

He turned away then, not trusting himself to remain. Tyrone, his face bright with lies, smiling his con man's smile, could waste his sweet talk on the police.

It was important to remember that the man was a murderer.

By the pool, in her beach chair, a trusting smile on her lips, out like a light, was Elaine McCorkle. She had stooped again to folly but would live to tell about it.

THIRTY-SEVEN

IN THE WEEKS that followed Roger Dowling was often reminded by Phil Keegan that if Tyrone Pajakowski had not stolen the St. Hilary's minibus, it was doubtful that any arrest would have taken place at the Easy Times Inn when the police arrived.

"That was a smart move, pinning him in the office."

"I wish that had been my intention."

"It made that woman call the police." Phil laughed, dismissing what he took to be diffidence, but Roger Dowling was not sure what had been in his mind when he drove the bus toward the office. Had he thought he could block the door by parking in front of it?

"Elaine slept through all the excitement."

"He had laced her drink with Valium."

"Her drink was full of Valium," Phil corrected. He was being a purist, eschewing guesses about causes, but he could not bait the pastor of St. Hilary's.

"Like Walter's malted."

"And Ron Pucceto in Vegas," Cy added. The media had feasted on the connection between Stacey, Marvin Wilson, and the Las Vegas mob figure.

Phil Keegan waved his cigar. Such facts had only become important later. "Thank God he stole the minibus."

Tyrone had now become the darling of the media. His lawyer encouraged him to tell all and a lengthy biography began to appear in the *Fox River Tribune*. Soon it was being syndicated around the country. Tyrone was featured on a television show devoted to unsolved mysteries. He willingly discussed the murders with the interviewer, whose concerned smile and solicitous manner infuriated Marie Murkin.

"Look at her! The man's a murderer and she fawns all over him."

Elaine had gone back to work for Phil Keegan. Her photographs in accounts of Tyrone's doings convinced her to diet seriously and she now weighed considerably less than she had. Marie Murkin had begun a novena to St. Ann on Elaine's behalf. That Elaine had been within minutes of drowning in the pool of the Easy Times Inn fascinated the housekeeper.

"Thank God you put two and two together, Father."

"Thank God he stole the minibus," Phil Keegan said again.

"I don't see why he wanted to kill Elaine," Cy Horvath said. He was on his second helping of Marie Murkin's goulash, which was endorsement indeed.

"Why did he kill Walter?" Marie demanded. "Or Marvin Wilson? Or the gambler in Nevada?" She looked sternly at the men eating the luncheon she had prepared for them. Father Dowling had commemorated the soul of Walter at the noon mass from which they had just come. "I'll tell you why. He was possessed!"

Marie nodded into the silence and then marched off to her kitchen.

Motivation was not the strong point of the story that Tyrone told the press. The most reporters got from him was an enigmatic smile when they asked why he had done it.

"Money," Stacey Wilson said. She sat in the front parlor on the edge of her chair. "The card he took from my purse told him where he could get one hundred thirty-five thousand dollars."

"Is this it?"

She examined the card he gave her. "Where did you get this?"

"It was what he wanted from Elaine. He copied the numbers and then returned it to her but must have thought better of it. He could not have her remembering that card."

"Money," Stacey said. In prison she had been plain, but now she seemed gaudy, heavy with makeup, elaborate earrings, necklaces, bracelets, rings asparkle. "I have everything now, because of what Tyrone did, but there's nothing I can do to help him. The trial won't take long the way he's blabbing. Why doesn't he keep quiet?"

"Perhaps he's trying to snatch victory from the jaws of defeat."

She waited for him to say more, but Roger Dowling let it go. In Tyrone's own telling of events, her son sounded very much in control. But he had murdered in vain and no amount of braggadocio could change that.

Amos Cadbury marveled at the fact that he and the police had duplicated one another's efforts in tracing the past of Stacey Pajakowski Jones Wilson and discovering that she had borne a son.

"I did not know the young man had made that claim to Captain Keegan's secretary."

"Your client is out in the cold?"

"In California? Hardly. He had no need of the money. I think much less of myself for having agreed to act for him."

Tuttle at least had come out of recent events with a profit. He was currently running a series of television ads, soliciting business, alluding to his role in the solution of the Marvin Wilson murder.

"The man is a disgrace," Amos said, shaking his head. But he could not keep a smile from his lips.

Marvin Wilson's widow was a wealthy woman now. She certainly had no intention of telling her story to the world. Fear of reprisals from Las Vegas remained, yet Stacey had no desire to flee to Europe.

"The only place I ever really liked was Vegas."

"Go to Monte Carlo."

"Oh, I couldn't."

"Why not?"

"After what happened to Princess Grace?" She shuddered.

That night Father Dowling sat up late in his studio, smoking his pipe, and considering the odd shrines and patrons and rituals that defined the life of Tyrone Pajakowski's mother. Roulette and baccarat were her rites, Las Vegas her place of pilgrimage, celebrities her saints. And greed had made the desert bloom.